Jane Yolen

Jody Lee

Merle Insinga

THE NESFA PRESS

BOSKONE XXIX

Storyteller

Jane Yolen

THE NESFA PRESS
BOX G, MIT BRANCH P.O.
CAMBRIDGE, MA 02139-0910
1992

FIRST EDITION

Library of Congress Catalog Card Number: 91-67894

International Standard Book Number:
0-915368-49-8 (Regular Edition)
0-915368-97-8 (Slipcased Edition)

This is a limited edition of 1000, of which 8 are a lettered and
slipcased edition, the first 200 numbered are an autographed and
slipcased edition, and the remaining are numbered.

This is book __185__

Copyright Acknowledgments

Contents

Jane Yolen:
An Introduction to
the Platonic Table
and
Other Household Items

by Patricia McKillip

I bought my first book by Jane Yolen, *The Girl Who Cried Flowers and Other Tales*, at some tender age when the possibility of meeting a real live author seemed as remote as bumping into the Queen of England at McDonald's. Now, some twenty-odd years later, I know that writers occupy space in time. They live in houses, not the ether; they speak more than pearls and abstract metaphysical nuts; they can be found in libraries, airports, hotels, bars, in bookstores signing books, at conventions, such as the Fantasy Con at the Claremont Hotel in Berkeley, where destiny took me one fateful day to find Jane sitting on someone's bed and discussing — as memory serves — cover art. The True Jane, as opposed to the Platonic Jane (that awesome being who exists nowhere but whose work is everywhere) appeared in her earthly form as a bright, funny, shrewd woman interested in everyone and everything to do with the business of storytelling.

Jane's picture books — of which are multitudes — seem to leap off the shelves of bookstores into your fingers. They are wondrous confections of art and fairytale. She pares language, character, plot to their simplest and most essential elements, and still surprises the reader with wonder. Even her titles tell stories: *Dream Weaver*, *Brothers of the Wind*, *The Boy Who Had*

Wings. We recognize these people, we remember them from some distant past, we begin to hear their stories even before we begin to read them. It's not surprising that her picture books topple onto our heads, insinuate themselves into our hands, and make us whisper, glassy-eyed and helpless, "Well, maybe just one more…"

She has also written collections of stories (*Tales of Wonder*), poetry, science fiction (*Cards of Grief, The Pit Dragon Trilogy*), longer works of fantasy (*Sister Light, Sister Dark*), and, recently, the YA novel that won the Jewish Book Council Award: *The Devil's Arithmetic*. It's a rare novel that brings tears to my eyes — magicians know one another's tricks. This one crept under my critical guard to twist my heart. Jane has also edited collections of stories for young adults, of fantasy, horror, and science fiction, among them *Dragons and Dreams*, and *2041*, where she managed to coax YA s/f out of the likes of Connie Willis and Joe Haldeman (and me). Her awards are becoming as numerous as her books. She has won the World Fantasy Award (for being Special), the Caldecott Medal (*Owl Moon*), the Golden Kite Award (*The Girl Who Cried Flowers*), the 1984 Mythopoeic Society Award (*Cards of Grief*), the Christopher Medal (*The Seeing Stick*), the Kerlan Award (for having more manuscripts than anyone else to donate to the Kerlan Collection), the Agatha Christie Award (for writing more books than Agatha Christie), the Airlines of America Award (for keeping them all in business), and the Mother of the Year Award (for being President of SFWA).

Rumors of Jane abound: that she causes brilliant and otherwise caustic writers to bring their teddy bears to her late-night storytelling sessions at conventions; that Revlon has been after her for years to reveal the secret of her perpetually youthful complexion; that she secretly writes songs for the rock and roll group Altamatum. I cannot answer for the rumors, but I do have my memories...

Of Jane miraculously dropping out of the sky over Wheaton, IL, to liven up a convention where I was dutifully plodding through my GoH duties.

Of Jane driving a motley crew in an old station wagon from a convention in Providence to Staten Island.

Of the house on Staten Island, where I graciously gave up the couch so she wouldn't have to sleep on the floor, only to have her complain that I snored. (I don't snore, Jane. I suspire.)

Of Jane at her house in Hatfield, surrounded by people celebrating her birthday, unwrapping something scant and lacy and illegal even between consenting adults.

Of Jane on a panel in Seattle giving a cultural analysis of the color pink.

Of Jane at a banquet in Florida, pretending to be a cockroach.

Of Jane and the Woolly Mammoth.

Of Jane in Minneapolis, Berkeley, Providence, Fort Lauderdale, Boston, Tucson, Sacramento, Chicago — in short, so many places that I must conclude conclusively that there are indeed two Janes: the Platonic Jane, who is Elsewhere, writing the hundred and umpteenth book; and the True Jane, who is, at any given moment, Somewhere on a panel discussing fantasy.

As well as hitting the road in her spare time for the sake of her art, Jane edits her own line of books for Harcourt, Brace, Jovanovich, and has written scholarly and critical works on children's literature. At a time when much of society has become wary of imagination and of the effects of fantasy on the young, she champions constantly and fearlessly the wonder and magic inherent in childhood. In the sprawling galaxies of both children's literature, with its conferences, classrooms, librarians, artists, and teachers; and of science fiction and fantasy, with its conventions, costumes, bar-sessions, no-holds-barred writers, and its general aura of disreputable revolution, Jane is well known, highly respected, well loved.

Corrections,
Emendations,
and
Footnotes
by Jane Yolen

1. I drove the Motley Crew from Staten Island to New Haven, where we went to the World Fantasy Convention. Said Motley Crew consisted of Pat, Robin McKinley, Terri Windling, and me. Among others.

2. Tomie dePaola has given more manuscripts to the Kerlan Collection than anyone else. He also has more money than I have. (More years and more pounds, too. But who's counting?)

3. The rock group Pat is thinking of may have been my sons' garage band Armageddon ("Music That Makes Mom Think It's The End of the World") or Cats Laughing or even Poetic Justice, all bands that have used my material. Or maybe not. Maybe she has a spyglass into the future. Pat has things like that.

4. She really does snore, whatever she wants to call it.

Storyteller

This began as a speech, one of thirty or forty I give each year, and mutated into an essay published in the British sf magazine Foundation. *It is all true. Would I lie to you?*

The Profession of Science Fiction, 37: The Author as Hero

When I first became obsessed with myth and folklore, I came upon Joseph Campbell's *The Hero with a Thousand Faces* and I underlined my copy with regular pen strokes, certain I understood it all.

Recently I had need to take it out again, because of an introduction to a major folklore collection I was working on, and I was amused at the temerity of my underlinings and the frequent exclamation points in the margins. Over the intervening years, I had become familiar with (literally) thousands of stories and tales. Rereading Campbell, I realized that I understood him less and admired him more than I had fifteen years ago.

His well-delineated hero pattern of *separation*, *adventure*, *return* was still clear to me. But what surprised me was that he never mentioned in his powerfully-drawn thesis what had become an overriding issue to me: that the writer of fantasy and fairy tales or that folklore of the future — science fiction — undergoes the same journey as the hero with every new story. And that venture astonishes me.

Imagine: I, still slightly overweight and approaching fifty, burdened by adolescent children and a mortgage, with a husband who is an academic and a fifteen-acre New England farm, am a hero. (I hate the word *heroine*, sounding as it does like a combination of a drug and lesser force. And I positively abhor Maya Angelou's proffered substitute, the coined word *shero* which ignores etymology.) That I, who prefer the comforts of home, loving adventures on vacations only, might be a traveler along Joseph Campbell's path of mythic destiny is a delicious irony.

However, try looking at it as I do. Campbell says this:

> A hero ventures forth from the world of common day into a region of supernatural wonder: fabulous forces are there encountered and a decisive victory is won: the hero comes back from this mysterious adventure with the power to bestow boons on his fellow man.

The literary mind jumps immediately to Jason and the Golden Fleece, Prometheus and fire, Arthur and the sword in the stone. The child reader remembers Dorothy and her magic slippers, Frodo and the ring, even Winnie Foster and the bottle filled with the water of life. We count our heroes with Campbell's coup stick.

But remember — it is the author who made that journey first. *A hero ventures forth from the world of common day...*

And what is more common than my attic writing room? Piles of unanswered mail, unfiled letters, stacks of books on the Real Soon Now shelf, the bills-of-the-month waiting to be paid, mounds of research volumes from the last novel written. My husband calls it my "private nuclear holocaust" and a reporter who visited said rather politely in her story about me that "Jane Yolen's filing system is erratic at best." Yet this is my very common day we are talking about, where ideas I have not yet had time to explore are put in a folder marked prosaically *Ideas* and left to stew for years. Where the opening lines of twenty-plus books await a more propitious time. (Just *what* was I thinking about when I wrote *I was anchored over that wonderful city, Venice, where the water lapped the housestairs like a tamed beast until a hundred years before I was born*?) Where the bulletin board over my desk is cluttered with family photos, bookmarks, a cartoon that reads "All of us here at Bobolink Books feel you have written the Great American Novel, ages four to seven," a quote from an old Vermont tombstone "It is a fearful thing to love what death can touch" which I put up seventeen years ago after my mother died, and a snapshot of the Malaysian merman I took in a small antique shop in Greenwich, England. Where memorabilia of a half-life in writing (I was a published poet in college, a journalist and then an editor after college, sold my first book when I was 22 and didn't know any better) sit on every shelf. Where a variety of stuffed animals hang from the rafters (a red dragon, a flying unicorn, a mermaid with shells for breasts) or squat on the bookcases (a selchie, a collection of space-faring toads). Common is common, though what I find commonplace may seem very odd to somebody else.

A hero ventures forth from the world of common day into a region of supernatural wonder… which is where I travel when I take these common day images and spin them into fantasies. For example: the Vermont tombstone ended up in a novel called *Cards of Grief* in which a guild of space-going anthropologists explore a planet where grieving is the highest art, a book I began when my father, dying a long, slow death from Parkinson's, moved in with us, lingering for four difficult years. Mourning became an art in our family indeed. For example: the merman swam rather nastily into a story called "The Malaysian Mer," a story set in Greenwich, England, but starring a middle-aged and middle class New England matron who also happens to be a magic wielder. For example: the red dragon was the cornerstone for my Pit Dragon Trilogy in which a boy, who looked remarkably like my oldest son Adam, wins his freedom from the system of bond slavery by raising and training a dragon to be a great fighter all by himself. Adam, who is essentially a loner who likes the illusion of doing everything by himself, *is* Jakkin. That my father or my son recognized themselves on the pages did not matter. They are and they are not those characters. Just as I was and was not the storyteller/poetmaker in *Cards of Grief* or the matronly Mrs. Stambley fighting a malicious merman in a Greenwich shop. The pages of literary fantasies are regions for all of us to be daring explorers of the dream landscape. Here the author is both the hero and the spirit guide.

A hero ventures forth from the world of common day into a region of supernatural wonder: fabulous forces are there encountered... well, orcs and gorgons and deathstars come immediately to mind. But as an author I think about the real fabulous forces, that infect the creative and creating mind: the untamed images, the half-formed ideas, the cluttered dreamscape, "the monsters of the id" as one old sf movie had it. The Gross National Product of Faerie which every author has to sort through and organize and understand in order to make a story live, be original, and True.

If you have never really looked at an author's first draft, you have no idea how an author battles chaos, how an author finds the jewel in the toad's eye, spins gold from flax, and all the other transformative metaphors.

Would you know, for example, that the following sentence about the dragon in my story "Dragonfield": *His name, in the old tongue, was Arredd and he was as red as blood,* so ordinary, so lacking in pizazz, would go through at least seven different metamorphic handlings and emerge in the end as: *His name in the old tongue was Arredd and his color a dull red. It was not the red of hollyberry or the red of the wild flowering trillium, but the red of a man's life-blood spilled out upon the sand.*

Every sentence in every story becomes a battleground filled with fabulous forces (as well as landmines, snipers, and tanks over the next hill) for the caring writer.

A hero ventures forth from the world of common day into a region of supernatural wonder: fabulous forces are there encountered and a decisive victory won: and that victory is, of course, the book set down whole.

It always astounds me that l am more tired after a day's long work at the typewriter, inventing and re-inventing, than I would have been doing hard physical labor. And I *have* done such labor: working with the Quakers building an outdoor education center one summer, picking oranges and grapefruit in a kibbutz one long spring, keeping an enormous farm garden and putting up a freezer-full of vegetables for seven years. But now that I understand the hero part, I can smile my hero smile and let the astonishment go. After all, didn't God rest on the seventh day, exhausted from his mind's labor? The author is surely a minor god, creating literary worlds which, though certainly less complex or prolix than the one in which we live (seriously, have you read the magazines *Natural History* or *Scientific American* cover to cover for a year?), are tiring creations nonetheless. Authors can only suggest the enormous complexity of a real world — and it takes us much longer than seven days!

A hero ventures forth from the world of common day into a region of supernatural wonder: fabulous forces are there encountered and a decisive victory won: the hero comes back from this mysterious adventure with the power to bestow boons on his fellow man.

Boons? It is but one small letter that stands between boon and book. One tiny magical transformation.

I stand before you, my only sword my pen, my only magic that which I hold in my mouth. Words — words have an incredible transforming power, the power to turn and to turn on. Stories contain all that is human magic. No wonder dictators and tyrants burn books and murder the story tellers.

And it is no wonder I love to write. How else would an almost fifty-year-old, slightly overweight Jewish mother get to be a hero?

I began this poem at Mariette Hartley's house. (We had been best friends in high school and remained friends all these years.) I worked on it on the set of her TV show. I finished it on the plane home. Mariette sent me a calligraphed copy for Christmas which hangs in my writing room. I gave Steve Brust a calligraphed copy of the last lines because he loves it. Pete Godwin insisted on printing it in a book of his. Poetry makes strange bedfellows.

The Storyteller

He unpacks his bag of tales
with fingers quick
as a weaver's
picking the weft threads,
threading the warp.
Watch his fingers.
Watch his lips
speaking the old, familiar words:

> "Once there was
> and there was not,
> oh, best beloved,
> when the world was filled with wishes
> the way the sea is filled with fishes…"

All those threads
pulling us back
to another world, another time
when goosegirls married well
and frogs could rhyme,
when maids spoke syllables of pearl
and stepmothers came to grief.

Belief is the warp
and the sharp-picked pattern
of motif
reminds us that Araby
is not so far;
that the pleasure dome
of a Baghdad caliph
sits side by side
with the rush-roofed home
of a Tattercoat or an animal bride.

Cinderella wears a shoe
first fitted in the East
where her prince —
no more a beast
than the usual run of royal son —
measures her nobility
by the lotus foot,
so many inches to the reign.
Then the slipper made glass
by a slip of ear and tongue.
All tales are mistakes
made true by the telling.

The watching eye takes in the hue,
the listening ear the word,
but all they comprehend is Art.
A story must be worn again
before the magic garment
fits the ready heart.

The storyteller is done.
He packs his bag.
But watch his fingers
and his lips.
It is the oldest feat
of prestidigitation.
What you saw,
what you heard,
was equal to a new Creation.

The colors blur,
time is now.
He speaks his final piece
before his final bow:

> "It is all true,
> it is not true.
> The more I tell you,
> The more I shall lie.
> What is story
> but jesting Pilate's cry.
> I am not paid to tell you the
> truth."

First published in my collection Dream Weaver, *this story is definitely an answer to Virginia Kirkus reviews, one of which said my stories were polished bijoux. I had to look it up, since I thought a bijou was a movie theater. It's not; it's a tawdry jewel. Further, the reviewer said that my tales were perfectly crafted, flawless in execution, and soulless. This story was my reply.*

The Pot Child

There was once an ill-humored potter who lived all alone and made his way by shaping clay into cups and bowls and urns. His pots were colored with the tones of the earth, and on their sides he painted all creatures excepting man.

"For there was never a human I liked well enough to share my house and my life with," said the bitter old man.

But one day, when the potter was known throughout the land for his sharp tongue as well as his pots, and so old that even death might have come as a friend, he sat down and on the side of a large bisque urn he drew a child.

The child was without flaw in the outline, and so the potter colored in its form with earth glazes: rutile for the body and cobalt blue for the eyes. And to the potter's practiced eye, the figure on the pot was perfect.

So he put the pot into the kiln, closed up the door with bricks, and set the flame.

Slowly the fires burned. And within the kiln the glazes matured and turned their proper tones.

It was a full day and a night before the firing was done. And a full day and a night before the kiln had cooled. And it was a full day and a night before the old potter dared unbrick the kiln door. For the pot child was his masterpiece, of this he was sure.

At last, though, he could put it off no longer. He took down the kiln door, reached in, and removed the urn.

Slowly he felt along the pot's side. It was smooth and still warm. He set the pot on the ground and walked around it, nodding his head as he went.

The child on the pot was so lifelike, it seemed to follow him with its lapis eyes. Its skin was a pearly yellow-white, and each hair on its head like beaten gold.

So the old potter squatted down before the urn, examining the figure closely, checking it for cracks and flaws, But there were none. He drew in his breath at the child's beauty and thought to himself, "*There* is one I might like well enough." And when he expelled his breath again, he blew directly on the image's lips.

At that, the pot child sighed and stepped off the urn.

Well, this so startled the old man, that he fell back into the dust.

After a while, though, the potter saw that the pot child was waiting for him to speak. So he stood up and in a brusque tone said, "Well, then, come here. Let me look at you."

The child ran over to him and, ignoring his tone, put its arms around his waist, and whispered "Father" in a high sweet voice.

This so startled the old man that he was speechless for the first time in his life. And as he could not find the words to tell the child to go, it stayed. Yet after a day, when he had found the words, the potter knew he could not utter them for the child's perfect face and figure had enchanted him.

When the potter worked or ate or slept, the child was by his side, speaking when spoken to but otherwise still. It was a pot child, after all, and not a real child. It did not join him in his work but was content to watch. When other people came to the old man's shop, the child stepped back onto the urn and did not move. Only the potter knew it was alive.

One day several famous people came to the potter's shop. He showed them all around, grudgingly, touching one pot and then another. He answered their questions in a voice that was crusty and hard. But they knew his reputation and did not answer back.

At last they came to the urn.

The old man stood before it and sighed. It was such an uncharacteristic sound that the people looked at him strangely. But the potter did not notice. He simply stood for a moment more, then said, "This is the Pot Child. It is my masterpiece. I shall never make another one so fine."

He moved away, and one woman said after him. "It *is* good." But turning to her companions, she added in a low voice, "But it is *too* perfect for me."

A man with her agreed. "It lacks something," he whispered back.

The woman thought a moment. "It has no heart," she said. "That is what is wrong."

"It has no soul," he amended.

They nodded at each other and turned away from the urn. The woman picked out several small bowls, and, paying for them, she and the others went away.

No sooner were the people out of sight than the pot child stepped down from the urn.

"Father," the pot child asked, "what is a heart?"

"A vastly overrated part of the body," said the old man gruffly. He turned to work the clay on his wheel.

"Then," thought the pot child, "I am better off without one." It watched as the clay grew first tall and then wide between the potter's knowing palms. It hesitated asking another question, but at last could bear it no longer.

"And what is a soul, Father?" asked the pot child. "Why did you not draw one on me when you made me on the urn?"

The potter looked up in surprise. "Draw one? No one can draw a soul."

The child's disappointment was so profound, the potter added, "A man's body is like a pot, which does not disclose what is inside. Only when the pot is poured, do we see its contents. Only when a man acts, do we know what kind of soul he has."

The pot child seemed happy with that explanation, and the potter went back to his work. But over the next few weeks the child continually got in his way. When the potter worked the clay, the pot child tried to bring him water to keep the clay moist. But it spilled the water and the potter pushed the child away.

When the potter carried the unfired pots to the kiln, the pot child tried to carry some, too. But it dropped the pots, and many were shattered. The potter started to cry out in anger, bit his tongue, and was still.

When the potter went to fire the kiln, the pot child tried to light the flame. Instead, it blew out the fire.

At last the potter cried, "You heartless thing. Leave me to do my work. It is all I have. How am I to keep body and soul together when I am so plagued by you?"

At these words, the pot child sat down in the dirt, covered its face, and wept. Its tiny body heaved so with its sobs that the potter feared it would break in two. His crusty old heart softened, and he went over to the pot child and said, "There, child. I did not mean to shout so. What is it that ails you?"

The pot child looked up. "Oh, my Father, I know I have no heart. But that is a vastly overrated part of the body. Still, I was trying to show how I was growing a soul."

The old man looked startled for a minute, but then, recalling their conversation of many weeks before, he said "My poor pot child, no one can *grow* a soul. It is there from birth." He touched the child lightly on the head.

The potter had meant to console the child, but at that the child cried even harder than before. Drops sprang from its eyes and ran down its cheeks like blue glaze. "Then I shall never have a soul," the pot child cried. "For I was not born but made."

Seeing how the child suffered, the old man took a deep breath. And when he let it out again, he said, "Child, as I made you, now I will make you a promise. When I die, you shall have *my* soul for then I shall no longer need it."

"Oh, then I will be truly happy," said the pot child, slipping its little hand gratefully into the old man's. It did not see the look of pain that crossed the old man's face. But when it looked up at him and smiled, the old man could not help but smile back.

That very night, under the watchful eyes of the pot child, the potter wrote out his will. It was a simple paper, but it took a long time to compose for words did not come easily to the old man. Yet as he wrote, he felt surprisingly lightened. And the pot child smiled at him all the while. At last, after many scratchings out, it was done. The potter read the paper aloud to the pot child.

"It is good," said the pot child. "You do not suppose I will have long to wait for my soul?"

The old man laughed. "Not long, child."

And then the old man slept, tired after the late night's labor. But he had been so busy writing, he had forgotten to bank his fire, and in the darkest part of the night, the flames went out.

In the morning the shop was ice cold, and so was the old man. He did not waken, and without him, the pot child could not move from its shelf.

Later in the day, when the first customers arrived, they found the old man. And beneath his cold fingers lay a piece of paper that said:

When I am dead, place my body in my kiln and
light the flames. And when I am nothing but
ashes, let those ashes be placed inside the Pot
Child. For I would be one, body and soul, with
the earth I have worked.

So it was done as the potter wished. And when the kiln was
opened up, the people of the town placed the ashes in the ice-
cold urn.

At the touch of the hot ashes, the pot cracked: once across
the breast of the child and two small fissures under its eyes.

"What a shame," said the people to one another on seeing
that. "We should have waited until the ashes cooled."

Yet the pot was still so beautiful, and the old potter so well
known, that the urn was placed at once in a museum. Many
people came to gaze on it.

One of those was the woman who had seen the pot that day
so long ago at the shop.

"Why, look," she said to her companions. "It is the pot the
old man called his masterpiece. It *is* good. But I like it even
better now with those small cracks."

"Yes," said one of her companions, "it was too perfect
before."

"Now the pot child has real character," said the woman. "It
has...heart."

"Yes," added the same companion, "it has soul."

And they spoke so loudly that all the people around them
heard. The story of their conversation was printed and repeated
throughout the land, and everyone who went by the pot
stopped and murmured, as if part of a ritual, "Look at that pot
child. It has such heart. It has such soul."

So there I was at a World Fantasy Convention. My editor, Terri Windling, said: "I want you to come out to dinner tonight with a group of new young Minneapolis writers." What author turns down a free meal? They were an adorable lot, so eager and tail wagging, I immediately dubbed them "The Puppies." (Terri called them The Beavers because of how hard they all worked — and how incessantly.) Emma Bull and Will Shetterly and Steve Brust and Pat Wrede and Pamela Dean and Kara Dalkey and probably others. "Would you, would you play in our universe?" they asked. They meant Liavek. Their enthusiasm was contagious. I said yes — and the next week an enormous "Bible" of the world — all the facts and figures and GNP of Liavek — fell out of my mail box into my hands. Who could take this seriously? I mean their Bible was longer than any stories I write. I'd show them — I'd get rid of them. I wrote "The Inn..." with its oily storyteller and ended up being the only person with a story or poem in each of the five Liavek volumes. Emma and I even — one slightly drunken evening (which means I had one half a glass of wine; I'm a cheap date) — made up a Liavek anthem. All I remember of it is: "Oh Liavek, oh Liavek,/Thy writers they all write on spec,/And we don't write that other drek/(TM)/Oh Lia-Liavek." It had been a long evening.

The Inn of the Demon Camel

It was in this very place, my lords, my ladies, during the reign of the Levar Ozle the Crooked Back, two hundred years to this very day (the year 3117 for those of you whose fingers limit the counting), that the great bull camel, afterwards known as The Demon, was born.

Oh, he was an unprepossessing calf, hardly humped, and with a wandering left eye. (You must remember that eye, Excellencies.)

The master of the calf was a bleak-spirited little man, an innkeeper the color of camel dung, who would have sold the little beast if he could. But who wanted such a burden? So instead of selling the calf, his master whipped him. It was meant to be training, my Magnificencies, but as any follower of the Way knows, the whip is a crooked teacher. What that little calf learned was not what his master taught.

And he grew. How he grew. From Buds to Flowers, he developed a hump the size of a wine grape. From Flowers to Meadows, the grape became a gourd. It took from Meadows all the way till Fog and Frost, but the hump became a heap and he had legs and feet — and teeth — to match. And that wandering left eye. (You *must* remember that eye, my Eminences.)

Without a hump he was simply a small camel with a tendency to balk. With the grape hump he was a medium-sized camel who loved to grind his teeth. With the gourd hump, he was a large camel with a vicious spitting range. But with the heap — O, my Graces — and the wandering eye (you *must* remember that eye) the camel was a veritable demon and so Demon became his name.

And is it not written in *The Book of the Twin Forces* that one may be born with a fitting name or one may grow to fit the name one is born with? You may, yourselves, puzzle out the way of The Demon's name, for I touch upon that no more.

It came to pass, therefore, that the innkeeper owned a great bull camel of intolerably nasty disposition: too stringy to eat, too temperamental to drive, too infamous to sell, too ugly to breed. But since it was a camel, and a man's worth is measured in the number of camels he owns and oxen he pastures and horses he rides, the innkeeper would not kill the beast outright.

There happened one day, this very day in fact, 195 years to this very day during the reign of Levar Tinzli the Cleft Chinned (3122 for those of you whose toes limit the counting), that three unrelated strangers came to stay at the inn. One was a bald ship's captain who had lost his ship (and consequently his hair) upon the Eel Island rocks. One was a broken-nosed young farmer come south to join the Levar's Guard. And one was an overfed mendicant priest who wore a white turban in which was set a jewel as black and shiny and ripe as a grape.

Was not the innkeeper abustle then in the oily manner of his tribe! He bowed a hundred obeisances to the priest, for the black jewel promised a high gratuity. He bowed half a hundred obeisances to the farmer, for his letter of introduction to the Guards promised compensations to come. And he bowed a quarter-hundred obeisances to the ship's captain because riches in the past can sometimes be a guarantee of riches later on. Thus did the innkeeper count his profits, not into the palm but into the future. As you know, Graciousnesses, it is not always a safe method of tabulation.

They ignored the innkeeper's flatteries and demanded rooms, which he managed to turn up at once, his inn being neither on Rose Row nor favored by such worthies as yourselves. He served his guests an execrable meal of fishless stew and an excellent mountain wine, the one cancelling the other, and so they passed the night, their new-forged friendships made agreeable by the inn's well-stocked cellar. Thus lullabied by strong drink, the three slept until nearly noon.

Now perhaps all that followed would not have, had it not occurred on the seventeenth day of Buds, for it was the very day on which four of the five mentioned in our story had been born, though they recognized it not.

The captain, who had been birthed that day forty years in the past, did not believe in such birth luck, trusting only to his own skill — which is perhaps why he had fetched up so promptly on the shoals of the Eel.

The young farmer was an orphan who had been found on a doorstep some twenty years past, and so had never really known his true birth day. His foster parents counted it five days after the seventeenth, the morning they had tripped over his basket and thus smashed the infant's nose.

And the priest, who had been born some sixty years in the past, had been given a new birth date by the master of his faith, who had tried, in this way, to twist luck to his own ends.

So that was three. But I *did* say four. And it is not of the innkeeper I now speak, for he knew full well his luck day was the twenty-seventh of Wind. But he had forgot that the bull camel, The Demon, humped and with the wandering eye (you *must* remember that eye, Exultancies), had emerged head first and spitting five years ago to that very day.

An animal casts no luck, neither good nor bad, you say, my Supremacies? And where is that bit of wisdom writ? Believe me when I tell you that the seventeenth day of Buds was the source of the problem. I have no reason to lie.

So there they were, three birth days sequestered and snoring under the one inn roof and the fourth feeding on straw in the stable. Together they invented the rest of my small tale and invested it with the worst of ill luck, which led to the haunting of the place from that day on.

It happened in this manner, Preeminencies, and, pray, you *must* remember that wandering eye.

The sun glinting on the roof of the Levar's palace pierced the gloom of the inn and woke our five on that fateful day in Buds. The camel was up first, stretching, spitting, chewing loudly, and complaining. But as he was tucked away in the stable, no one heard him. Next up was the innkeeper, stretching, grimacing, creaking loudly, and complaining to himself. Then in order of descending age, the three guests arose — first the priest, then the captain, and last the farmer. All stretching, sighing, scratching loudly, and complaining to the innkeeper about the fleas.

They gathered for a desultory breakfast and, as it was a lovely day, one of the lambent mornings in Buds when the air is soft and full of bright promise, that meal was served outdoors under a red-striped awning next to the stable.

The camel, ignoring the presence of ox and ass, chose to stick his head into the human conversation, and so the concatenation began.

The three guests were sitting at the table, a round table, with a basket of sweet bread between them, a small crock of butter imprinted with the insignia of the inn to one side, and to the other a steaming urn of kaf, dark and heady, and a small pitcher of milk.

The talk turned to magic.

"I do not believe in it," spake the captain.

"I am not sure," said the farmer.

"Believe me, I know," the mendicant priest put in and at that same moment turned his head toward the right to look at a plate of fresh raw shellfish that had been deposited there.

Now that placed his head — and atop it the turban with the jewel, black and shiny and ripe as a grape — slightly below the camel's nose, and it, great protuberance that it was, sensitive to every movement and smell carried by the soft air of Buds.

Well, the turban tickled the nose; the camel, insulted, spat; the priest slapped the beast, who snapped back at the priest's hand.

But you did not — I hope, Ascendencies — forget that wandering eye?

For the camel's eye caused him to miss the offending hand and snap up the black jewel instead.

At which the priest fainted. Then rallied. Then fainted again, clutching his chest and emitting a scream rather like that of a Tichenese woman in labor: "*Ee-eah, ee-eah, ee-eee-ehai.*"

The captain leaped to his feet, upsetting the table, bread, butter, shellfish, milk, and kaf, and drawing his knife. The farmer simultaneously unsheathed his sword, a farewell gift from his parents. The innkeeper hovered over the priest, fanning him with a dirty apron. And the camel gulped and rolled his wandering eye.

At that, the priest sat up. "The jewel," he gasped. "It contains the magic of my master."

To which sentence the captain responded by knifing the camel in the front. This so startled the farmer, he sunk his sword into the camel up to its hilt from behind. The priest fell back, screamlessly, into his faint. The innkeeper began to weep over his bleeding beast. And the camel closed his wandering eye and died. Of course by his death the luck — such as it was — was freed.

And do you think, Extremities, by this the tale is now done? It is only halfway finished for, in the course of the telling, I have told you only what *seemed* to have happened, not that which, in actuality, occurred.

The priest at last revived and offered this explanation. The master of his faith, a magician of great power but little ambition, had invested his luck in a necklace of ten black jewels which he distributed to his nine followers (it was a *very* small sect). He kept but one jewel for himself. Then each year, the nine members of the faith traveled the roads of Liavek letting the master's magic reach out and touch someone. But now, with a tenth of his master's luck swallowed and — with the camel's death — freed, there was no knowing what might happen.

On hearing this, the innkeeper began to scrabble through the remains of his camel like a soothsayer through entrails. But all he could find in the stomach was a compote of nuts, grains, olives, grape seeds, and a damp and bedraggled feather off the hat of a whore who had recently plied her trade at his hostelry.

"No jewel," he said at last with a sigh.

"Probably crushed to powder when the luck was freed," said the farmer.

"Then if there is no jewel," said the captain, "where is this supposed luck? I told you I did not believe in it."

At which very moment, the severed remains of the camel began to shimmer and reattach themselves, ligament to limb, muscle to bone; and with a final *snap* as loud as a thunderclap, the reanimation stood and opened its eyes. The one eye was sane. But the wandering eye, Benevolencies, was as black and shiny and ripe as a grape and orbited like a malevolent star 'round elliptic and uncharted galaxies.

The four men departed the premises at once in a tangle of arms, legs, and screams. The innkeeper, not an hour later, sold his inn to a developer, sight unseen, who desired to level it for an even larger hostelry. The priest converted within the day to the Red Faith, where he rose quickly through the ranks to a minor, minor functionary. The farmer joined the Levar's Guard, where he was given a far better sword with which he wounded himself serving the Levar Modzi of the Flat Dome.

And the captain — well, he sold the jewel, black and shiny and ripe as a grape, which he had stolen from the turban the night before and replaced with an olive because he did not believe in magic but he certainly believed in money. He bought himself a new ship, which he sailed quite carefully around the shoals of the Eel. There had been no luck in the jewel after all, for the priest's master had had as little skill as ambition, no luck except that which a sly man could convert to coin.

Then what of the camel? Had his revival been a trick? Oh, there had been luck there, freed by his death, which had occurred at the exact day and hour and minute five years after his birth. But the luck had been in the whore's feather, which she had taken from a drunken mage who had bound his magic in it, creating a talisman of great sexual potency. So the demon camel, that walking boneyard, ravaged the inn site and impregnated a hundred and twenty local camels — and one very surprised mare — before the magic dwindled and the ghostly demon fell apart into a collection of rotted parts. But those camels sired by him still haunt this particular place: spitting, chomping, reproducing, and getting into one kind of mischief after another.

And each and every one of those little demons, Tremendousies, is marked by a wandering eye.

The story of Daedalus and Icarus has fascinated me for years. It has everything in it: murder, intrigue in high places, lust, monsters, hubris, the death of a child…in other words, a typical Greek myth. I changed things around a bit. Okay — I changed things around a lot. (Previously I had written an Icarus poem which was published in Parabola *with a Barry Moser illustration, the first of our collaborations. I have written a children's picture book called W ings with pictures by Dennis Nolan. And I won the Daedalus Award for a body of short fantasy fiction. Or maybe I won it for a short fantastic body…nah, that's not quite it. This particular myth, however, consumes me.)*

Sun/Flight

They call me the nameless one. My mother was the sea, and the sun itself fathered me. I was born fully clothed and on my boyish cheeks the beginnings of a beard. Whoever I was, wherever I came from, had been washed from me by the waves in which I was found.

And so I have made many pasts for myself. A honey-colored mother cradling me. A father with his beard short and shaped like a Minoan spade. Sisters and brothers have I gifted myself. And a home that smelled of fresh-strewn reeds and olives ripening on the trees. Sometimes I make myself a king's son, godborn, a javelin in my hand and a smear of honeycake on my lips. Other times I am a craftsman's child, with a length of golden string threaded around my thumbs. Or the son of a *dmos*, a serf, my back arched over the furrows where little birds search for seeds like farmers counting the crop. With no remembered pasts, I can pick a different one each day to suit my mood, to cater my need.

But most of the time I think myself the child of the birds, for when the fishermen pulled me up from the sea, drowned of my past, I clutched a single feather in my hand. The feather was golden, sun-colored, and when it dried it was tufted with yellow rays. I carried it with me always, my talisman, my token back across the Styx. No one knew what bird had carried this feather in its wing or tail. The shaft is strong and white and the barbs soft. The little fingers of down are no color at all; they change with the changing light.

So I am no-name, son of no-bird, pulled from the waters of the sea north and east of Delos, too far for swimming, my only sail the feather in my hand.

The head of the fishermen who rescued me was a morose man called Talos who would have spoken more had he no tongue at all. But he was a good man, for all that he was silent. He gave me advice but once, and had I listened then, I would not be here, now, in a cold and dark cavern listening to voices from my unremembered past and fearing the rising of the sun.

When Talos plucked me from the water, he wrung me out with hands that were horned from work. He made no comment at all about my own hands, whose softness the water-wrinkles could not disguise. He brought me home to his childless wife. She spread honey-balm on my burns, for my back and right side were seared as if I had been drawn from the flames instead of from the sea. The puckered scars along my side are still testimony to that fire. Talos was convinced I had come from the wreckage of a burning ship, though no sails or spars were ever found. But the only fire I could recall was red and round as the sun.

Of fire and water was I made, Talos' wife said. Her tongue ran before her thoughts always. She spoke twice, once for herself and once for her speechless husband. "Of sun and sea, my only child," she would say, fondly stroking my wine-dark hair, touching the feather I kept pinned to my *chiton*. "Bird child. A gift of the sky, a gift from the sea."

So I stayed with them. Indeed, where else could I, still a boy, go? And they were content. Except for the scar seaming my side, I was thought handsome. And my fingers were clever with memories of their own. They could make things of which I had no conscious knowledge: miniature buildings of strange design, with passages that turned back upon themselves; a mechanical bull-man that could move about and roar when wound with a hand-carved key.

"Fingers from the gods," Talos' wife said. "Such fingers. Your father must have been Hephaestus, though you have Apollo's face." And she added god after god to my siring, a litany that comforted her until Talos' warning grunt stemmed the rising tide of her words.

At last my good looks and my clever fingers brought me to the attention of the local lord, I the nameless one, the child of sun and sea and sky. That lord was called Circinus. He had many slaves and many bondsmen, but only one daughter, Perdix.

She was an ox-eyed beauty, with a long neck. Her slim, boyish body, her straight, narrow nose, reminded me somehow of my time before the waves, though I could not quite say how. Her name was sighed from every man's lips, but no one dared speak it aloud.

Lord Circinus asked for my services and, reluctantly, Talos and his wife let me go. He merely nodded a slow acceptance. She wept all over my shoulder before I left, a second drowning. But I, eager to show the Lord Circinus my skills, paid them scant attention.

It was then that Talos unlocked his few words for me.

"Do not fly too high, my son," he said. And like his wife, repeated himself. "Do not fly too high."

He meant Perdix, of course, for he had seen my eyes on her.

But I was just newly conscious of my body's desires. I could not, did not listen.

That was how I came into Lord Circinus' household, bringing nothing but the clothes I wore, the feather of my past, and the strange talent that lived in my hands. In Lord Circinus' house I was given a sleeping room and a workroom and leave to set the pattern of my days.

Work was my joy and my excuse. I began simply, making clay-headed dolls, with wooden trunks and jointed limbs, testing out the tools that Circinus gave me. But soon I moved away from such childish things and constructed a dancing floor of such intricately mazed panels of wood, I was rewarded with a pocket of gold.

I never looked boldly upon the Lady Perdix. It was not my place. But I glanced longways, from the corners of my eyes. And somehow she must have known. For it was not long before she found my workroom and came to tease me with her boy's body and quick tongue. Like my stepfather Talos, I had no magic in my answers, only in my fingers, and Perdix always laughed at me twice: once for my slow speech and once for the quick flush that quickly burned my cheeks after each exchange.

I recall the first time she came upon me as I worked on a mechanical bird that could fly in short bursts towards the sun. She entered the workroom and stood by my side watching for a while. Then she put her right hand over mine. I could feel the heat from her hand burn me, all the way up my arm, though this burning left no visible scar.

"My Lady," I said. So I had been instructed to address her. She was a year younger than I. "It is said that a woman should wait upon a man's moves."

"If that were so," she answered swiftly, "all women would be called Penelope. But I would have woven a different ending to *that* particular tale." She laughed. "Too much waiting without an eye upon her, makes a maid mad."

Her wordy cleverness confounded me and I blushed. But she lifted her hand from mine and, still laughing, left the room.

It was a week before she returned. I did not even hear her enter, but when I turned around she was sitting on the floor with her skirts rolled halfway up her thighs. Her tanned legs flashed unmistakable signals at me that I dared not answer.

"Do you think it better to wait for a god or wait upon a man?" she asked, as if a week had not come between her last words and these.

I mumbled something about a man having but one form and a god many, and concluded lamely that perhaps, then, waiting for a god would be more interesting.

"Oh, yes," she said, "many girls have waited for a god to come. But not I. Men can be made gods, you know."

I did not know, and confessed it.

"My cousin Danae," she said, "said that great Zeus had come into her lap in a shower of gold. But I suspect it was a more mundane lover. After all, it has happened many times before that a man has showered gold into a girl's skirts and she opens her legs to him. That does not make *him* a god, or his coming gold." She laughed that familiar low laugh and added under her breath, "Cousin Danae always did have a quick answer for her mistakes."

"Like you, my Lady?" I asked.

She answered me with a smile and stood up slowly. As I watched, she walked towards me, stopping only inches away. I could scarcely breathe. She took the feather off the workbench where it lay among my tools and ran it down my chest. I was dressed only in a linen loincloth, my *chiton* set aside, for it was summer and very very hot.

I must have sighed. I know I bit my lip. And then she

dropped the feather and it fluttered slowly to the floor. She used her fingers in the feather's place, and they were infinitely more knowing than my own. They found the pattern of my scar and traced it slowly as a blind child traces the raised fable on a vase.

I stepped through the last bit of space between us and put my arms around her as if I were fitting the last piece of my puzzle into a maze. For a moment we stood as still as any frieze; then she pushed me backwards and I tumbled down. But I held on to her, and she fell on top of me, fitting her mouth to mine.

Perdix came to my room that night, and the next I went to hers. And she made me a god. And so it continued night after night, a pattern as complicated as any I could devise, and as simple, too. I could not conceive of it ending.

But end it did.

One night she did not tap lightly at my door and slip in, a shadow in a night of shadows. I thought perhaps her moon time had come, until the next morning in the hallway near my workroom when I saw her whisper into the ear of a new slave. He had skin almost as dark as the wings of the bittern, and wild black hair. His nostrils flared like a beast's. Perdix placed her hand on his shoulder and turned him to face me. When I flushed with anger and with pain, they both laughed, he taking his cue from her, a scant beat behind.

Night could not come fast enough to hide my shame. I lay on my couch and thought I slept. A dream voice from the labyrinth that is my past cried out to me, in dark and brutish tones. I rose, not knowing I rose, and took my carving knife in hand. Wrapped only in night's cloak, the feather stuck in my hair, I crept down the corridors of the house.

I sniffed the still air. I listened for every sound. And then I heard it truly, the monster from my dream, agonizing over its meal. It screamed and moaned and panted and wept, but the tears that fell from its bullish head were as red as human blood.

I saw it, I tell you, in her room crouched over her, devouring my lady, my lost Perdix. My knife was ready, and I fell upon its back, black Minotaur of my devising. But it slid from the bed and melted away in the darkness, and my blade found her waiting heart instead.

She made no sound above a sigh.

My clever fingers, so nimble, so fast, could not hold the wound together, could not seam it closed. She seemed to be leaking away through my clumsy hands.

Then I heard a rush of wings, as if her soul had flown from the room. And I knew I had to fly after her and fetch her back before she left this world forever. So I took the feather from my hair and, dipping it into the red ocean of her life, printed great bloody wings, feathered tracings, along my shoulders and down my arms. And I flew high, high after her and fell into the bright searing light of dawn.

When they found me in the morning, by her bedside, crouched naked by her corpse, scarred with her blood, they took me, all unprotesting, to Lord Circinus. He had me thrown into this dark cave.

Tomorrow, before the sun comes again, I will be brought from this place and tied to a post sunk in the sand.

Oh, the cleverness of it, the cleverness. It might have been devised by my own little darling, my Perdix, for her father never had her wit. The post is at a place beyond the high water mark and I will be bound to it at the ebb. All morning my father, the sun, will burn me, and my mother, the rising tide, will melt the red feathers of blood that decorate my chest and arms and side. And I will watch myself go back into the waters from which I was first pulled, nameless but alive.

Of fire and water I came, to fire and water I return. Talos was right. I flew too high. Truly there is no second fooling of the Fates.

MERLE
INSINGA
1991

This poem is really for my husband. There is no truth to the rumor that he is a beast.

Beauty and the Beast:
An Anniversary

It is winter now,
and the roses are blooming again,
their petals bright against the snow.
My father died last April;
my sisters no longer write,
except at the turning of the year,
content with their fine houses
and their grandchildren.
Beast and I
putter in the gardens
and walk slowly on the forest paths.
He is graying
around the muzzle
and I have silver combs
to match my hair.
I have no regrets.
None.
Though sometimes I do wonder
what sounds children
might have made
running across the marble halls,
swinging from the birches
over the roses
in the snow.

When Parke (Pete) Godwin asked me for a story for his anthology Invitation to Camelot, *I had already begun this one. It was to be part of a projected book of my own called* Guinevere's Booke, *a companion to* Merlin's Booke. *The original publisher was not interested, however. A plague on such decisions. Of the three or four stories I had started, this was the first one I finished because Pete wanted it.*

Meditation in a Whitethorn Tree

I am a man much abused by women, a thing set spinning on the wheels of their ambitions. Three women betrayed me during my overlong and lonely life, though the betrayals were not what I thought at the time. And the only one I accused of treachery, my Niniane, nymph of the darkling woods, she was none of those three.

Niniane, woodsgirl, your sweet sorcery did not betray me but rather be-treed me, if an old man may be allowed a small joke. Yet if you had not, I would never have had the time to come to this self-knowledge. There was always too much else to do than to indulge my vanity. Running a kingdom takes many hours of hard work; running a king takes even longer. But time moves slowly within the trunk of a tree, as sluggish as winter sap or the blood in an old man's veins. I have had many years of this slow time to think about my past. I have no future but this whitethorn cask.

So I will rehearse the stories of the three, that the very wood may bear witness to my witlessness. It is no small irony that a man renowned for his wisdom should, in fact, be the greatest fool in all Christendom.

1
Igraine

Who has not heard her story? When she is spoke of, it is as Gorlois' lovely wife, beguiled by the wicked machinations of a mage, the victim of a wizard's plot.

Victim! She was never such a gull. It was she tempted Uther, poor, dumb, besotted brute; tempted him — and used me.

I remember the very moment they met. Indeed how could I forget? He told me of it often enough thereafter, or at least what he remembered of it. What he remembered and what *was* were nowhere the same. Love lays a mist on memory. But wizards deal in such moments. We turn them into crystals and store them in the cabinet of the mind.

Igraine had been much talked of that year in the rooms where men gather and speak of harlots and happiness in a single breath. She was a beauty, no doubt of it: gold hair, green eyes. It was as if dark hair and dark eyes held no fascination for them, so limited were their collective imaginings. She was the season's darling and men — when they are driven to it — can spin romances as silken and fine as any village granny.

So word came of her to Uther long before he gazed upon her. He was tempted by the portraits his men drew in the air. He was, shall we say, prepared for his passion as meat, long in a marinade, is prepared for the heat.

The golden beauty and the thickened, middle-aged, battle-scarred king. Who would have guessed it? He had no manners, except with a sword. He could not dance without a horse beneath him. He was as blunt and as brutal as a mace. Who would have guessed it indeed.

But Igraine had. She was tired of the strong winds, the lofty folds of cliff, the narrow roadway, the stony beaches, the cold waves of Tintagel. She wearied of the duke's same stories, the repetition of faces, the rota of Cornish ways. Such familiarity wilts even the loveliest of flowers. Some women thrive on the strange, the brutal, the obscene. She begged for a month at the court, but Gorlois wanted her rooted only in Cornwall like some wild, beautiful hedge rose planted in a pot. Besides, he coveted kingship and made war upon the king.

I had all this from Igraine's serving woman who had escaped to the east to beg a love philter from me. Often I exchanged magical gifts for gossip, which is the common coin of magery.

The serving woman leaned over the stew I had cooked for her, drinking in the smells of love, and turning to me with eyes as narrow as needles. "But how can my lady come to court when her husband is at war with Uther?"

I did not then hear the play on her words. I reserved all such trickery to myself. Fool that I was, fool that I am. I replied to her, *"What was is not necessarily what is."* How we mages love obfuscation. Then I added, that she take my meaning exactly, "Truces can be made in a day."

It was not a month later that Gorlois sued for peace and was invited to Uther's castle for the Easter coronation feast. Women have much more to do with war than warriors, believe me.

I thought Igraine would be happy just to see the new faces at court, but she came dressed for seduction in a gown that would have been daring even on a whore. Yet it had an innocence, too, lent it by ribbons and lace.

Uther came to my chamber that same night, his face flushed and angry.

"I want her," he said heavily, undoing the clasp at his neck as he slumped into the great wooden chair by my bedside. "I want Igraine." Uther was always direct; it was his greatest virtue and his greatest fault. One always knew where one stood with him. In a plowman that is a good thing, in a king it is not.

"You have just signed a truce with her husband," I pointed out. "After months of trouble from the west your kingdom is now secure. He is your liege man; he has sworn fealty. It is simply not good form to seduce his wife."

"I do not want to seduce her," Uther said bluntly. "I want to take her and make her my own."

I spent another fruitless hour trying to counsel him, but he left with desire unchecked and I fell to sleep. Or at least I tried to sleep. Uther stormed back into my room less than an hour later, his face like a Cornish sky, troubled and dark.

He roared, "They have left me, gone secretly, without my leave."

"Who?" I asked, afraid I knew.

"Gorlois has stolen her from me."

"She was not yours to steal."

It did no good. He would be neither comforted nor controlled and we were back at war within the hour. Within days Uther had troops ravaging the ducal lands, but he had no great success of it, except for the good men slaughtered on both sides, which is the legacy of any war, whatever the cause. The duke had taken to his castle Terrabyl and left Igraine in the safer house, Tintagel, where she could be guarded easily by placing soldiers across the narrow ridge of land.

Uther became a raging bear. What work there was in the newly formed kingdom — taxes and truces and the ordinary seasonal rounds — were all left undone. Farmboys were yanked from the fields to serve in the army. Farm wives were conscripted to serve as cooks and camp followers. Plows were turned into swords. And I knew that unless I intervened decisively, there would be neither crops nor kingdom come the fall. So I suggested magic, albeit reluctantly, for the consequences of such magic are often hard to bear.

"Glamour," I said to the king when he had interrupted my sleep for the third time one night with reports of the ongoing war. "You need a bit of glamour to win this lady."

"I need more men, not magic," he said. "Gorlois is a fox but I...I am a dragon. I will swallow him alive and I *will* have her."

But I would not leave him alone. I played the same tune again and again that night until he was finally forced to dance to it. At last, if only to shut me up, he agreed. My plan was a simple one. With magic it is best not to be too complex. I would cast his features and mine as Gorlois and his faithful Jordanus. We would ride thus disguised past guards and gates and he would — I promised him — sleep that night with Igraine.

"But I want her to love *me*, not that simpering dukeling. *Me*, for myself." His coarse features twisted in a parody of passion.

And then I knew things were more treacherous than I had thought. I had hoped he would make a quick sweaty night of it, his face the duke's, his loins — that was another matter altogether. I could not counterfeit what I had not seen. But my master wanted more, and more my magic might not stand. If I turned him into Gorlois' twin for more than a night, well, that kind of glamour carried its own danger. He might never again wear the face of the king. And Britain needed *this* man, brutal and frank though he was. That was well writ in the stars, that he carry the kingdom for fifteen years yet. What would rule instead of him would be chaos, or so the firmament warned. I did not believe the prophesies of crystal balls or the fuzzy omens told by cards. But the skies over our green land did not lie.

"You shall have her," I said, my heart heavy with the promise. *One step at a time*, I chided myself. "So prepare yourself to ride, my lord. Unarmed."

"Unarmed?" Uther had not ridden unarmed since he was a babe.

"Cold steel will pierce the glamour. You must be unarmed

that your face may carry another's features."

He nodded and left to get ready. And I? I leaned out of the window to look once more at the stars. I saw a kind of swirling passion writ there. And then without warning, a comet blazed across the sky. It meant a birth or a death. Or both. The stars do not lie, but they do not give up their secrets easily. I would have to think on that bright light. Praying for the birth. I went down the stairs to meet my king.

We rode through that night and the next and another to Tintagel, and in a forest near the headland where the castle sat, we made a small fireless camp. It was there, under the night sky, ablaze with information for those who could read it, I cast the glamour that turned Uther into the likeness of Gorlois and myself into Jordanus. Uther did not believe anything had happened, so subtle are the traceries of glamour, until he turned and saw my face.

"The likeness is uncanny —" he began. Then he stopped. And laughed. The change had made him quicker with words as well, just like Gorlois.

"We can remain but a night with these features imprinted upon our own," I warned. "Or we risk becoming that self, though but a shadow of the living man."

He nodded, plainly unhappy with it, but also understanding faster than ever Uther had in his own face.

And so we were swept into Tintagel, across the narrow conjunction, under the banners of Cornwall, and no one dared stop our march, for they believed us to be the duke and his best friend riding homeward. So men read one another, by the face and not the heart.

Igraine met us by the great gate, having been warned by some minion or another. She was dressed more plainly than in court, but that did not change her beauty. Indeed, it only enhanced it. She dropped us a small courtesy, and then opened her arms. Uther drove into them, his passion the only thing not counterfeit.

I saw the surprise on Igraine's face, and then a kind of strange transformation as she struggled to control her mouth. I did not read it right at the time, thinking she was not as much in love with her duke as he with her.

"My lord," she said, and she stared over his shoulder at me.

I put my finger alongside my nose, a gesture Jordanus used habitually to signal understanding or compliance or consideration. Perhaps I was a beat too slow, my own body still aware of its own rhythms, so different from the form it now wore.

"My lord," Igraine said again, looking deeply into Uther's eyes. "I have longed for your embrace." And then she drew him swiftly into her bed chamber and locked the door behind.

*   *   *

We left in the morning, the king and I, though I moved with more grace. In him the two forms were already warring. As we went out through the portcullis on our horses, I turned my head and saw his features shift suddenly, as if the glamour were readjusting itself. I felt a corresponding tremor in my own limbs.

"We must hurry, Uther," I whispered urgently, leaning over to slap at the horse's broad flank.

We leaped away and galloped down the path. I felt a burning in my breast, as if I had recently eaten of some tainted meat. And a strange lightheadedness. I knew what it meant: both Jordanus and Gorlois were dead, killed I supposed in the early morning fighting. If we wore their features for an hour more, we would *become* them. I did not wait for the forest this time. I turned our horses onto a small path and there, almost within sight of Tintagel and its guards, I spoke the words that would bring us back the familiarity of our own features.

As I watched Uther's face, it seemed to cloud for a moment, and then the rough-hewn, broken-nosed homely king looked out at me, his eyes cloudy with lack of sleep.

"Her husband is dead and so you must be alive in your own body and face to be her suitor now."

"Suitor?" His voice was more weary than puzzled.

"Do you not still want her?"

He shook his head. I understood. She had proved herself only a woman in bed, not an angel, not a fairy queen. Then I remembered the comet. A death. But something in me said that these small deaths, Gorlois and Jordanus, were not what the blaze portended. A birth!

"She bears a child," I said, suddenly sure of it. "Your child. Your *son*."

That caught him. "A son!" he said. For all his rutting, his women had only borne him girls. "Then I must marry her."

"So you shall," I said. "I will arrange it."

Thus it was that Igraine became a queen and a mother within short months of one another. And as I bore the child away, my part in that unholy bargain, though I had not known of it at the time, Igraine looked up at me and laughed.

Oh, the tale tellers and the tale bearers say she screamed at me, begging me to return the boy. But it was not that kind of scream at all. It was a cry of triumph, for she had gotten it all, her heart's one desire: a king, a kingdom, and a crown.

2
Morgaine

The second woman to betray me was but a child at the time. I thought I had a way with children. What magician does not? We are but a few fingers from every child's laughter. A coin behind one ear, a flower from the other, a card plucked out of the air with ease, and the child is ours.

So I charmed Morgaine on our first meeting, the day her mother and Uther were wed. She needed much charming, her father lately dead, her mother married to a stranger. The coin I took from behind her right ear was a copper I let her keep. The flower from the left was a speedwell the color of my eyes. The card was the Ace of Death. I should have been warned, for the Eastern cards, though difficult to read, rarely lie, but I was too enchanted by her childish wit.

She said, "Are you to be my uncle, then?"

"If you wish," I answered, "though I am no relation to the king."

"But I heard my mother say that your relationship to Uther was too close for her liking."

I had to laugh at that. "Then I shall be your uncle indeed," I said, as I handed her the card.

The day after the wedding she found me in my tower room. The door was shut though not locked, and any adult would have respected its meaning. But Morgaine, being but five or six years old at the time, was a curious child. A locked door was simply more the challenge. She fiddled with the latch and pushed the door open, then stood trembling in the doorway, smiling. I thought at the time she trembled with fear, but now I know it was with anticipation.

When I heard the noise, I looked up and smiled back at her.

She was such a slight, spindly thing then, her plaited hair the color of an old penny, not quite brown and not quite copper. Her eyes were a muddy gold; the left had a spot of green in it, the right a spot of grey which gave her a somewhat daft look when she willed it. Many a man was to be taken off guard by that expression. She had a smudge on her nose and a gap between her upper front teeth. They say such a gap portends licentious-ness, but who would ever think it of a child.

"Hello, Uncle," she said; even then her voice was low and cozening, with a husky quality that was much remarked on when she was a child.

"I am busy, Morgaine," I said. "I have no time to play with you today."

She looked at me carefully with those particolored eyes. Her face was deadly serious. I thought it a joke at the time. "Oh, I am not here to play, Uncle. I am here to learn."

Who was to guess she knew full well what she meant? I sighed and signaled her into the room, warning her that I would dismiss her if she troubled me but once.

She scrambled up onto a stool by my side and sat there so quietly for the rest of the day, it was as if no child at all were in the room. I know now how unnatural that was, but you see I had only known children in groups and she was like no child before or since.

She came often after that, sitting still as a stone on the stool by my side, watching me work in my laboratorium, asking no questions but sometimes imitating in a kind of passionate mime what I did with my hands and my mouth. She taught herself to read long before I realized it. Indeed, I thought she was still on her *alpha* and *bets*, her mother being a follower not of Jerome but of the White One. But the child had a mind of her own and was puzzling out my texts before I thought her aware of them. If she had asked questions, she would have known the truth of the magic — and its consequences. But she cared more for the form of it than the heart, and therein lay the doom she brought upon us all.

And I — the gods help me — thought her endearing. Even when she was full grown, a woman in form (though, alas, inside she was still a vengeful child, I see that now), I remembered her as the child she had been, my silent companion, my secret sharer. I did not see the simulacrum she had become. I forgave her her little sins. No, even worse, I *excused* them. And she knew me for the foolish dotard that I was, a drooling grandpap.

It was nearly two years after her mother's marriage and her brother's birth that Morgaine's first bout with the demons showed forth. We were all at a feast celebrating some god or another. When one is a king by the sword, as Uther was, it is always best to honor too many gods than too few.

Morgaine wore her plaits atop her head but otherwise showed no sign of womanhood. Unlike her mother, she was not an early blossom ripe and ready to fall into the first hand. It was Morgaine who elected herself to be Hebe to Uther's Zeus. She brought the great wooden goblet carved with entwined dragons to the table and set it before him.

Uther picked up the cup, smiled unconvincingly at Morgaine — whom he had never professed to love — drank two sips, and fell forward onto the table.

The hall grew deathly still, and the only sound was Morgaine's voice crying out "*Father*" in a high, sweet tone. Then she threw herself on top of him and wrapped her arms about him.

I should have known the falsity in her voice, which was a good octave above her normal tone. I should have noticed that she whispered as she held him. But I, like all the rest, mistook it for weeping, mistook her for a normal child. If I had read her lips, I would have known it for a deadly spell.

I ran to Uther, pulled him over on his back, pushed Morgaine away, and opened his shirt. Putting my ear to his chest, I heard the erratic beating of his heart. He smelled of wine and something sweet, something deadly. From my bosom I drew up a small golden flask containing *huantan*, the universal medicine that only comes from the East. I unstoppered it.

"Prise open his mouth," I roared.

Two men leaped to do my bidding.

I poured three drops into Uther's mouth, then closed his mouth with mine in the kiss of life. Breath for breath I gave him till he took it, swallowed, gasped, and moaned beneath me. Then I drew back and he sat up slowly.

The men cheered. Igraine, who had been sitting by his side the entire time stunned, her beautiful broad forehead beaded with sweat, gave a faint smile. Morgaine had disappeared.

"Who has done this?" Sir Ector said in a whisper more deadly than a roar. He took up the cup and sniffed it once, then held it over his head.

"Not Morgaine. Not my child," said the queen.

But we none of us believed it could be she. She was but eight or nine at the time. And so it was that the wine steward was hanged, for messages to him in Latin were found signed and sealed with the ring of a Western duke. That the steward could not read was never considered alibi enough. One can always find a reader in a court as large as Uther's.

Uther recovered but he was never again as strong as he had been. His enemies began to overrun the corners of the kingdom.

I knew that only the king himself might check their advances, and so we propped him up in a horse litter, filled with medicines that made his eyes glitter and his tongue a bit loose. And, like Moses in the Hebrew books, when we raised his arms, his army won. We returned him to Londinium and another feast.

Again the child brought him his cup, but this time he pushed it aside. Worried, I sniffed at it, but it was clean of any poisonous spell. However, the battle had taken its toll and Uther left the feast.

"Let me go to my father in his room," Morgaine insisted. "I will sing to him and rub his temples until he falls asleep."

And we all praised her daughterly concern, forgetting that though he was a father, he was none of hers.

In the morning Uther could neither speak nor sign with his hands, and on his temples were ten dark marks. If we could have read them as easily as a village witch reads palms, could we not have had a confession there?

For three days and three nights Uther lay in his stupor, neither awake nor asleep, neither alive nor dead. The castle was darkened and the servants walked with shoes muffled in cloth. Only Morgaine played with her dolls and sang brightly in the halls. But she was still so much a child, we excused her.

On the fourth day, as I sat by his side, Uther gave a bit of sound, like a rabbit caught in a trap. I pressed my ear to his mouth and he whispered to me.

"Morgaine," he said.

I thought he wanted to summon her, to thank her for her concern, so I called her in. She stood by his bedfoot and smiled, the kind one gives in a sickroom for encouragement. I marveled that a child should instinctively know what to do. But when I dream of it now, knowing what I know, it reminds me of her mother's smile, triumphant and sly.

"Morgaine," he said, his voice almost full. He struggled to sit up in bed and pointed his finger at her.

"For *my Father*," she said. And smiled again.

Uther said nothing more, but fell back with a bright red

foam on his lips.

When the men gathered and the priests and Igraine and her women, I told them that he had said more.

"He said that Arthur should rule after him. He said, 'On Arthur I bestow God's blessing and my own, and Arthur shall succeed to the throne of pain for forfeiting my blessing.'" No one questioned it. No one wondered that Uther on his deathbed should have been more articulate than ever in his life. And the only one who might have dared call me a liar was too young to be there to witness my small deceit. Yet it was no lie but rather Uther's dearest wish. I read it in his eyes as he died, as I had read it in the stars. The heir, however he is begat, is still the heir.

But the words Morgaine spoke as Uther lay there, his lips bright with foam and his eyes pleading with death for more time, haunt me to this day. I thought them strange when they were spoken, but I understand them now, now that I realize the depths of her betrayal.

She said, "I shall care for little Arthur, my lord, do not worry on that account. He shall be as you were, father and not father. I shall love him as more than a sister, though I am his sister but by half. I shall bind him to his kingdom forever."

And then she smiled, her mother's smile, a smile full of treachery and deceit, that I took only for childhood's end. But Uther, knowing that smile, died without being shriven.

3
Guinevere

The third who betrayed me was Arthur's own queen, though the betrayal was not what the storytellers believed.

She was never the beauty they sing of. Her hair was not gold but rather corn-colored. Her eyes were not green but gray. Her nose was too long and her mouth was too small and she had a dimple in her chin that, it was later said, was a cleft for the devil to hide in. She was neither tall nor small but of medium height and her bosom was certainly not one to make men swoon. Yet she could be serious in one breath and merry the next, and her voice was ever sweet and low. She had a genius for friendship — the making and the breaking of it. And best of all, her hips were well set apart the better for child-bearing, which is of course a great virtue in a queen.

She was the second daughter of a noble Roman who had fallen in love in the wild country of the Silures and went to live there against the caution of his family. Her sister, Gwenhwyach, was the first recommended to me when it was known I was on a search for our king. But Gwenhwyach, though infinitely more beautiful than her sister, was a silly wench given to fits of giggles and hiding her mouth behind her hand. Besides, she had the small hips of a well-bred Roman wife. A king needs an heir. So I looked at the second sister, Gwenhwyfar.

Unlike her older sister, who had the graces and the elliptical manner of her patrician father, Gwenhwyfar was always to the point.

"I would be a good wife to your king," she said to me. "I would bear him many sons and be a kind queen. My faithfulness to my lord and his land would never be questioned." She cocked her head to one side, a gesture I would come to know well, and laughed. "Besides," she said, "I can read and write in three languages — British, English, and Latin. I am learning Frank, slowly, because I may have need of it some day. I can play the Roman harp and sing passably, I never giggle, and" — she leaned towards me — "and I know the mathematics of wizardry."

Startled, I opened my eyes wide, which she took for a good sign. She could always read me better than I could read myself.

"I know," she said, laughing again, "that the very word *wizard* is itself mathematically pure. The W and the D are both in the fourth degree, the W fourth from the alphabet's end and the D fourth from its beginning. I and R stand in the ninth degree. Zed is the omega and A the alpha, and thus W-I-Z-A-R-D is a perfect word."

I had to laugh with her. "And what then is *Gwenhwyfar*?" I asked.

"Call me Gwenny," she said. "That is what my friends do."

As I said, a genius for friendship. And she was, besides Arthur, my one true friend. That is why it has taken me so long to believe that she betrayed me.

I recommended her without hesitation to the king. It was not that he was an unromantic sort, but kings must choose queens for their bloodlines and their holdings. Love can be found in any wench's bedroom. Breeding cannot.

Their wedding was one of proper pomp and all the dukes and barons left off quarreling and came. Morgaine, as the king's stepsister, was there as well, with her little dark-haired bastard. His mewling and puking nearly made a disaster of the day. But Gwenny shone. She even picked up the child and dandled it on her knee and only when it played with the pearls on her bodice did it leave off its cranky cries.

Arthur seemed different with Gwenny. *Guinevere* he called her, not being able to wrap his tongue around the wild Silurian name. He seemed not only content but, somehow, complete. When I looked at them together, I was filled with a kind of paternal pride, as if my choosing had made a circle where no circle had been before. Surely self-satisfaction is one of the larger sins, though it is not in any litany.

Month after month and month went by and Gwenny's belly did not swell. There is nothing less satisfying at a new court than a queen with a flat stomach. All the news of the day begins and ends there. It was spoke of more than the weather. Gossip filled the ears, wine the bladder, but nothing seemed to fill our Gwenhwyfar.

I begged a private audience with her.

"Gwenny," I said, for she ever insisted I call her that when we were alone, "your duty to the king and the kingdom is yet undone."

She placed her hands over her stomach and sighed. "It is not that he does not try," she said. "Sometimes five and six times a week. He groans and sweats and sounds like a stallion, but still my womb is tenantless."

I shook my head and handed her a small vial filled with a grey-green liquid the color of leaf mold. "Give him this to drink, but half, and you to take the rest."

She reached for it eagerly.

"Pour it out an hour before bed into two earthenware cups. Take it moments before he enters you," I said.

She looked down and blushed. Then she looked up again and stared deeply into my eyes. "I love him, you know. I did not expect that. I did not hope for that. Just to be treated well, as my father did my mother. Just to be valued and trusted. But I love him, for he is strong and gentle and kind and bright and the best of them all. Even if this were poison you bid me drink, I would drink it — for him. For Arthur."

I covered her hand with mine, the hand that held the vial. "It is neither poison nor a sop, but a tisane of periwinkle," I said. "It is to make you both more...more eager, so that the seed might ride high inside of you and touch that part which makes a child."

"We are already *eager*," she said, and laughed. "Sometimes night does not come soon enough."

I stood, bowed, and left, sweat running down my back. Talking of such matters to her made me extremely ill at ease, though only the gods knew why.

They consumed a tun of the stuff, and still it did no good. A year went by and then a second, and even Sir Kay came to talk to me of it. He had a filthy mouth and a cesspool for a mind, and the things he suggested would not have been fit for a sow, much less a queen. So I ignored him and read some of the forbidden herbals, where I learned nothing new, just marjoram for dropsy and brook-lime for St. Anthony's fire and alderberry for boils. But as Gwenny had none of these or the hundred more, my reading was of little use. Either the queen was barren or the king had no seed worth spilling or there was a curse on them so deep I could not read it in the stars. It was time for stronger medicine.

And so I went to her on an early spring day when the king and many of his men were in the woods to the west. We sat by a mullioned window and the sun dusted her shoulders like a golden shawl.

"The birds have returned, Gwenny," I said. "They are making their little nests." Indeed we could hear them outside, and one, a finch, was building above the window. A piece of straw hung down.

"You are here to speak to me again of an heir," she said.

"Can I never surprise you, Gwenny?"

"Merlin, you are a book whose runes can be read by anyone

who cares," she said. "And *I* care."

I knew I loved her then and could say what had to be said. "This time I shall surprise you, Gwenhwyfar."

She opened her grey eyes wide, and they were the color of the tidal river Tamar on an overcast day. "Using my Christian name? Are we not friends?"

"We are and we will be again, but you will not like what I have to say…" I faltered.

"Then say it quickly. It is best to be quick when the news is worst," she said. She reached out to hold my hand, which was trembling.

"The kingdom needs an heir. You *must* have a babe or the king will be forced to put you aside. And we both know how good you are for him and our land. So if Arthur cannot give you a child, you must discreetly find a man who can."

She pulled her hand away from mine in the roughest gesture I ever had of her. "Are you putting yourself forward as the candidate, then?" she asked.

This time it was I who was angry. "Gwenny, I am your friend. And Arthur's. I am old enough to have fathered you. And a mage cannot…must not…"

"It is true, then? You lose your magic if you are…no longer…perfect?" she asked, the words bitter in her mouth. "Tell me, mage, does the W fall off the beginning of *wizard*? Does the Zed wilt? Does the D…" and she gave a sign with her forefinger that I had seen only Sir Kay and his gross companions use, meaning a man's tool faltering. I had not known that ladies could know such things, much less use them.

"*Gwenhwyfar!*" I said, my voice a roar.

It sobered us both. She lowered her hands to her lap, folded them quietly, and kept her eyes fastened on the interlaced fingers.

"I mean you must seek out the most perfect knight in the

kingdom, whose body and heart are the equal of Arthur's."

"And whose loins are more than equal…" she whispered.

"And whose mouth will be silent with love for you," I said.

"You speak of Lancelot du Lac, of course."

I nodded.

She looked up suddenly and laughed. "I always knew my Frankish would be useful for something, though I never learned how to say 'Will you bed me now, my knight.' "

I said nothing.

"Is it truly the only way, Merlin?" she asked, her voice cracking twice on the short question.

"I have thought many hours and days and weeks and months on it," I said. "I have used all the magic I have, what knowledge of the body, all the tricks and sorceries. You have drunk and eaten all the herbal remedies and to no avail."

"To no avail," she echoed.

"I could…could help you…" I stuttered. Then I summoned up the courage to complete the thought. "I could put a glamour on Lancelot so that he looked like the king."

She shook her head. "I am no Igraine," she said, "to want to try and fool my heart. I either do it straight or do it not at all."

I breathed out very carefully and thought that she was, indeed, the truest, finest woman in the land.

"But I must do it at once. Today. Tonight. Tomorrow at the last. Else I will be able to do it never." She reached out and touched my hand. "But I do it because I love Arthur," she said. "And because I love you. Not because of Lancelot du Lac. Never because of him."

"I know," I answered. "I know."

What she did that night or the next or the next was not written down anywhere, not in her diary nor on her face. And I waited for word of it, and Lancelot began to sigh out loud, and the court was filled with the kind of gossip I had hoped would never start. But for all that, Gwenny's body did not change with the passing of the spring. And before I could speak to her again, Sir Kay and his company laid a trap. When it was sprung, the queen and her perfect knight lay in it.

"I do not believe it, Merlin," said Arthur. "I cannot believe it." His voice was an agony. I could not meet his eyes. "But they were found in bed."

"You said there was a sword between them."

"Any man can climb over steel lest he be a man of the fey. And any couple that lies with a sword between them, a man can bridge that gap with his own sword, be it ever so broad a blade." So he whipped himself, with words and with images. Image is but the beginning of imagination.

"Ask her," I said.

"I did," he replied.

"And what did she say?"

"Riddles. She spoke riddles. She said: 'If I sinned it was for the kingdom. If I did not it was for you. Either way I am condemned. Either way my life with you is forfeit. Trust me, dear heart.' And I did, and I do, but my heart is within my breast and the crown lies upon my head. I cannot keep her though I trust her. I cannot lie with her again though I love her. I cannot let her live though I die without her touch." He wept.

And I — I said nothing, for there was nothing left to say.

So Lancelot took her away, rescued her or stole her, depending upon your side of the fight. But it was I who planned it and who taught him his part. He was always just a sword in another man's hand.

She left him for a nunnery as soon as she could, for if she could not love Arthur she *could* love God. In her mind, I think, the two were one.

A note was delivered to me that I could not at that time

understand. It said, "The sword was true, as I was, to my heart and not to my head. Forgive me."

I did not know what it was she wanted forgiven, at least not then. But I know now. Oh, Gwenny, you could not bring yourself to sleep with another man though the kingdom called for it, you who drew the sword and kept it there all the long night for Arthur's sake, so willing to die with your name shamed throughout the land so that Arthur might be able to put you aside with anger and without remorse. Did you not realize that as much as you loved him, he loved you? Did you not know that without you he dies?

Oh, Gwenhwyfar, if you had trusted me, instead of telling Sir Kay's gossipy wife that you planned to lie with Lancelot that night so that you could be trapped. Why did you not just tell me no, and I would have looked for yet another solution. There are babes that can be bought in this great kingdom of ours. You might have even adopted your stepsister's child.

Igraine betrayed me out of love of power. Morgaine out of power and revenge. You betrayed me for so much less — and so much more. Why is it, sweet Gwenny, I find that the harder to bear?

Three women, and I a thing set spinning on fortune's wheel, I who thought myself the spinner.

Yet wait. Something in these tales rings false. Did I know so much? Did I know so little? Could an old man's memories be as muddled as time?

Niniane, woodsgirl, speak to me again. What did I know, what did I live, what did you spin out for me over the long wooden years?

Well, time and memory are all I have now. Let me consider these three once more. I will tell all the tales like beads on a chain, that some day I may know the truth of it. Some day.

Given as a call to arms at the opening of the 19th Society of Children's Books Writers (SCBW) conference, this speech was subsequently reprinted in both the SCBW and SFWA Bulletins. It was picked up by the Journal of the California Library Association and has been photocopied and mimeoed for classes in children's literature all over America. It also convinced ABC to do a story on the subject. A reporter for the show interviewed me for half an hour. ABC ended up using one line. I figure I still have fourteen minutes and a little more owing on my Fame Meter.

A Call to the Ramparts

Since the beginning of the SCBW conferences — some 19 years ago — it has been my duty and privilege, not to mention my hammy pleasure, to give the initial crowd-rousing speech whenever I have been a part of these four days. And over those years, I have talked about writing with joy, about writing for the child within, about writing with honesty, about the rewards (not monetary most of the time!), and about the discouragements when writing for children. I have tried to provide incentive, cheer, fortitude, and a touch of chicken soup.

But this year is different.

We are gathered here inside our fortress, my dear friends, while the Huns, the Vandals, and the Visigoths are at the gates. And it is not a question of whether you or I will survive the rejection letters, the slush pile, the remainders, the Kirkus reviews, or the Thor Power Tool Amendment. It is a question of whether literature — and quite specifically children's literature — will survive.

Let me tell you a story.

Once upon a time, a few years ago, in a city next to my town, a city known for its liberal views, the chief of police decided that he had a right to burn books. Not only burn them, but to make decisions about which books to burn. He did not read the books, mind you, but he skimmed them for words he considered inappropriate, insalubrious, in two syllables — DIR-TY.

He then made a list of those words and presented them at a press conference where he read the words out loud. Among the list of recognizable F and S words was one that especially made him furious. It was from *Manchild in the Promised Land*. The word was:

chitlins

Now, chitlins is a southern dish made from the small intestines of pigs. And while chitlins may be non-kosher, disgusting to look at, and — in my northern opinion — inedible, they are hardly obscene. I might not serve them at my own dinner table, but I certainly would not ban mention of them from a book.

We laughed at the police chief.

A few years later, a school board in another state banned a book, sight unseen, from its high school reading list. That book was called *Making It with Mademoiselle*. Only after the Home Ec teacher went to bat for the book, explaining that it was a pattern book from *Mademoiselle* magazine, was the book reinstated on the list.

We laughed at the school board.

In Nashua, New Hampshire, *Ms* magazine was removed from the high school shelves because a school committee member, who was also a member of the local John Birch Society, asserted that the magazine contributed to the "Communist Takeover of the USA as planned."

We laughed at the committee member.

In Jacksonville, Florida, a Christmas play was banned

because of the word "pregnant," which parents felt was too suggestive of sex education for elementary school playgoers. They did not, as far as I know, suggest a stork deliver the infant Jesus to the manger nor did they revise the story to include a cabbage patch.

We laughed at those parents.

In Eldon, Missouri, the local board of education banned the *American Heritage Dictionary* from the schools because it contained definitions of 39 naughty words. The complainant was a Missouri highway patrolman who — according to *The Newsletter on Intellectual Freedom* — said, "If people learn words like that, it ought to be where you and I learned them — in the streets and in the gutters."

We laughed at the patrolman.

In Lincolnton, North Carolina, a minister, discovering a book called *How Does It Feel? Exploring the World of Your Senses*, decided the book was "wicked, perverted and pornographic." He checked the book out of the library — and kept it. He says he intends to pay for it, but eight months later had not, though I suspect that in his Bible one of the Ten Commandments still reads, "Thou shalt not steal."

We laughed at that minister.

In Texas, led by country singer-turned-evangelist Penny Baker, a group of people burned collections of fairy tales including "Snow White," which Ms. Baker passionately accused of "introducing mirror gazing." That is surely one of the greatest sins of the world. She also noted, "There's a queen full of hate who turns herself into a wicked witch to destroy a teenager. That shows murder to me." I contend if she had read the ending of the story, where that wicked queen has to dance in red hot iron shoes until she drops down dead, that even Ms. Baker might have been satisfied that — at least in this instance — mirror gazing is not encouraged!

We laughed at that evangelist.

In Colorado, a school board banned *The Dictionary of American Slang* because a student's mother complained that she found him "chuckling over the dictionary."

At the Mark Twain High School in Missouri, *Huckleberry Finn* was banned at the behest of black parents who considered it racist. When the only honest, upright, moral adult in the book is black? Ironically, when the book first came out, it was condemned as being anti-racist. Mark Twain would have loved the irony.

From the *Wall Street Journal*, August 7, 1990, comes this chilling report:

"Staff at [Wilton Manors Elementary School] in South Florida…had written a musical called 'In Quest of Banjo Man' to help teach geography. Some 100 fifth graders were set to stage the tale of a starfish who crawls from continent to continent encountering a variety of cultures. That is, until parents of one student read and reread the script, carefully annotating what they saw as references to voodoo, paganism and devil worship. The parents noted, for instance, that the play mentions 33 countries in Europe, which multiplied by 2 is 66, one digit short of 'the Number of the Beast' — 666. These parents, supported by their pastor, took their complaint to the school principal *who cancelled the play*." (My italicizing.)

In Anaheim, California, all of Shakespeare's plays except *Hamlet* and *Romeo & Juliet* were banned, all of Dickens except *Oliver Twist*. *A Wrinkle in Time* and *The Lion, the Witch & the Wardrobe* were banned as anti-Christian and pagan. *Julie of the Wolves* was banned for its rape scene. *The Upstairs Room* was banned because it has 14 (count 'em) instances of the word "damn." Other books challenged or banned by parents and/or school boards have included *The Grapes of Wrath*, *The Catcher in the Rye*, *Brave New World*, *The Diary of Anne Frank*, *The*

Wizard of Oz, The Scarlet Letter, Little Red Riding Hood, and…oh, the list goes on and on.

Are we still laughing?

I wish I could say these are isolated incidents, but they are not. After awhile, they stop being funny because the roll call is — quite literally — endless. The results of such a litany on any thinking, caring, literate individual *has to be* depression. The banning of books has escalated so enormously in this country that after the second Reagan election, attempts to censor books in American libraries had more than tripled. The figures now six years later are too awful to be contemplated.

There is a book called *Ravaged by the New Age* by Texe Marrs, in which in a chapter entitled "Satan's Bookshelf" there is a four-page attack on such authors as Madeleine L'Engle, Shel Silverstein, and C.S. Lewis for occultism, anti-Christian sentiment, and bad words. The chapter insists that much of children's literature — and especially fantasy — is designed to encourage devil worship. Marrs' book is often cited by Funda-mentalist book banners who read it instead of the literature.

Book banning and book burning are not something new. In this country self-appointed moralists have always told us what we should and should not do, what we should and should not think, what we should and should not feel, view, listen to, or read.

In 1789, fiction *in general* was damned for being a corrupting influence on the young. At the same time, in the redoubtable *New England Primer*, which was filled with tidy moral lessons and phonics and the ABCs taught through Bible rhymes such as "In Adam's Fall we sinned all," there was a word list. It was the first instance of a word list ever put forth by American educators. These were words, mind you, that children were *supposed* to learn to read. The list included, among others, the words "vile" and "sloth" and "fornication."

One man's morals is another man's chitlins!

Banning books is, of course, one of the first things that a totalitarian government does. It sets up its own self-appointed censors and goes after the works of authors with whom it does not agree. Cardinal Richelieu once remarked sardonically, "Give me six lines written by the most honorable of men and I will find an excuse in them to hang him." Such hangings of men — and hangings of books — happened in the days of Rome, in the days of Hitler, in the Soviet Union — and to poor Salman Rushdie in hiding even as we speak.

That is why we cannot let it happen here. Not just in laughable incidents in Texas or Missouri or in Colorado or California or Massachusetts, but *anywhere*. As Kurt Vonnegut — one of the most frequently banned of American authors — has written, "The freedom to choose or reject ideas, to read books of our choice and to publish freely is the very bedrock of our free society."

In Ray Bradbury's classic novel about book burning in the future — *Fahrenheit 451* — Fire Captain Beatty describes how the books were burned: first by minorities, each ripping out an offending paragraph or page from this book or that, until the time finally came when the books — as well as the minds — were empty and closed. Ironically, *Fahrenheit 451* had been censored in much the same way, without Bradbury's knowledge, in its paperback edition. Slowly, over the years, during different reprintings of the book, some 75 separate sections — sometimes just one word, sometimes more — were snipped out. When he found this out, an outraged Bradbury had all the pieces restored.

Recently, Walden Books had ballots placed in an ad against censorship and available at the stores. So many thousands of people took the trouble to fill out the ballots that it took the sponsors weeks to count them all. That's the good news. The bad news is what is happening with the National Endowment for the Arts grants and the banning of music lyrics — abhorrent as they are — from stores. And the worst news of all is that the censorship of children's books continues apace. From a newspaper article just a few months ago in Seattle:

> *Witchcraft in the public schools?*
> *That's what some people think is happening in Anacortes, where a sometimes-bitter debate over a new reading series has divided the community.*
> *One citizen group has accused the Anacortes School District of replacing a traditional reading method with a kindergarten through sixth-grade Canadian-based reading series that encourages occultism.*

And what is the fingered story from the textbook that leads off the article? It is a story written in 1963 by a New York author that begins:

> *Isabel was a witch!*
> *At least she should have been a witch.*
> *Her mother was a witch. Her mother's mother was a witch. Her mother's mother was a witch.*
> *In fact, all her relatives back as far as she could remember had been witches, which, if you are a witch, is very far indeed.*

I was 22 when I wrote that. The book went through a number of editions and was popular in both hardcover and paper, though it is now out of print. Encouraging occultism? The story is a metaphor. It is about a witch (read: a little girl) who was different from the others and, in the end, as Witch

Hazel tells her "It's your difference that makes the difference." Isabel becomes important and well-liked in her community because she stands up for her differences. No — it doesn't teach witchcraft or occultism. Personally, I think anyone who sticks a knife into a toad saying, "Dicky-dicky-dembo," expecting the toad to turn into a dragon or a prince, has some serious nuts and bolts loose. But it does teach a — perhaps — even more dangerous lesson: that of valuing our differences.

A mind, I like to tell my young friends, is like a parachute. They both work best when open. And an open book equals an open mind.

It is a simple equation, that — OB=OM.

But the average adult American reads less than four books a year. And those four are probably fitness books, *Reader's Digest* condensed books, or Danielle Steele. We who write children's books, then, are on the front lines. We defend the castle. Outside, my dear friends, are the Huns, the Vandals, and the Visigoths.

You get the boiling oil. I'll nock the arrows. And we must all hope that the moat dragon does its work. Mixing metaphors and historical periods with great abandon, I am warning you and urging you and telling you *WE MUST BE READY*. The time for laughing is over. And Cassandra here is ready to fight. I hope you are, too.

I wrote this as a song, hoping my son Adam would set it to music for his band Cats Laughing. (Emma Bull was lead singer, Steve Brust drummer.) He never did.

Deirdre

She was a woman of wheat and sea,
A woman of corn and sky,
In whose eyes a man might live for long,
In whose eyes a man might die.
> So they died, they died, they died, and they died
> In the hour of their desire,
> For she was a woman of wheat and sea
> With a heart that was made of fire.

She was a woman of laughter and tears,
And she was a woman of night,
In whose thighs a man might rest for years,
From whose thighs he might take flight.
> So they ran, they ran, they ran, and they ran
> In the hour of their desire,
> For she was a woman of wheat and sea
> With a heart that was made of fire.

chorus:
> And all of Ulster mourns her still,
> And all of Ulster cries,
> And all of Ulster bleeds the years,
> And all of Ulster dies.

She was a woman of rose and briar,
A woman of snow and blood,
In whose heart a man might drown forever
Or float upon the flood.
        So they drowned, they drowned, they drowned,
                they burned,
        In the hour of their desire,
        For she was a woman of wheat and sea
        With a heart that was made of fire.

chorus:

        And all of Ulster mourns her still,
        And all of Ulster cries,
        And all of Ulster bleeds the years,
        And all of Ulster dies.

I read the most fascinating small bibliography of William Marshal —
The Flower of Chivalry *by Georges Duby — and this little story
thrust itself upon me. One of the things I love about being a writer
is getting to research oddments of history. But this one was not
research, I was home sick with my feet tucked under a lap robe and
a cup of tea by my side. I had picked up the book because it looked
interesting and was short enough to finish before the next round of
snuffling or coughing. I couldn't put it down until the end. Maybe
my story was a way of making Earl Marshal's story last longer.*

Feast of Souls

The old man is lying under a white cloak with a large red cross
emblazoned. Kneeling by his bed is a younger version of
himself, a dark-haired, hawk-nosed man, eyes carmined with
weeping. The bed is large and hung with heavy wine-colored
curtains, but they are pulled back to let in air and light. The old
man needs all the air and light he can get. He no longer eats
anything but a little mushroom crumbled in a bowl, sprinkled
with fresh-baked bread. And white wine. Red is too strong, he
has told them. It fires the blood.

There are always watchers in the bedroom now, the vigils
set by those who love him best, those who expect the most from
him. His son, this strong-beaked survivor, has organized the
relays. John d'Erley and Thomas Basset are there most often, by
their own requests. But it is the son, the Younger as he is called
by his mother and those of parallel quality, for he bears his
father's name, who takes the most perilous watch. Wrapped in
his silken gown, the squirrel collar soon to be replaced by his
father's sable, he sits late at night by the bed. His is the
midnight watch, those times when the Devil is most likely to
prowl and Death to visit.

Because we do not wish to be confused with those small demons that men are prone to number and to shun, we never visit the dying at night. We come to the bedsides at less vulnerable times. We *wish* to be seen. We *wish* to be known. To be counted, catalogued, wondered at. That is our charge, after all. We are the harbingers. We are the messengers. We sow a people's God that we may reap the harvest of their souls. How else to feed on this alien earth?

That is why the Monday before Ascension, during the day, we show ourselves to Earl Marshal as he lies dying. There is no satiety in feasting on small souls. We look for the men of nexus, the turning points of history, the great foci. And these we know from the histories. Not the ones writ centuries after, but the *chansons* and ballads, the journals and logs set down by the ones who loved them best and count their loss the greatest.

We knew from the histories that the earl's dying would be a long, slow progress. What began at Candlemas would last a full two months and more, taking him to Marlborough Castle, to Westminster, thence riding down his pain to London Tower, where he would wait, besieged behind the thick walls, as if waiting for some final charge by Death's minions. But then he retreated once again, this time by slow water to his manor in Caversham. Death, our brother, followed.

But we went before. In this eternity of feasting, we always go before. Death reads the histories, even as do we. He knows the times and the places, though he cannot come before time. He must hope to harvest what we have not yet happened upon. There are two of us and only one of him but he is a glutton. We are tasters; he takes all.

In 1219, in Earl Marshal's dark bedroom, we wear white so he may have no trouble discerning us in the gloom.

His son is begging him to eat. "We are certain," he says to his father in a voice he would never have used if the old man were not now permanently abed, "it will do you good." Just as reported in the histories.

The arrival of eternity has softened the earl. A man who captured some five hundred knights in his lifetime of tourneys, who sired five sons and five daughters upon a wealthy, willing wife, he is not used to listening to the importunings of his children, especially not to one called all his life The Younger. Still the earl has been made kind in this last crisis, in case he has to justify these last words to his god.

"Then for that," he answers in a voice made husky by fever, "I shall eat as much as I can." The histories are always word-perfect in these pasts. Perhaps it is that memory is greater when letters are not learned. Perhaps we reconstruct history out of story by traveling back in time. Perhaps our hunger for the feast of souls lets us listen with lenient ears. There are many *perhapses* that can be fashioned over centuries of feasting.

The Younger leaves to get the food, relieved, yet fearful that food really *will* sustain his father in his long dying. The squirrel collar tickles his neck, reminding him that it is not yet sable. The servants do not lower their eyes as quickly to him as they will when he is master.

Two men, the estimable John d'Erley, who has given up mansions and marriage to remain Marshal's squire, bound to him by the kind of love that men in this time enjoy but do not name, and Thomas Basset, that consummate cipher, raise the earl up so that he may sit while eating.

Basset leaves the room to collect the food from The Younger's own hands. There is still fear of poisoning; someone might want to hasten the Flower of Chivalry to his death. He must not be rushed before time.

D'Erley slips his hand behind the earl's back. The touch comforts them both, though neither will admit it. Especially d'Erley, who has more to lose by such an admission, having neither wife nor child nor cleric's collar to save him from calumnies.

I show myself to the earl, as does my companion. The white of our robes gleams in the dim lumens. He cannot count our limbs nor make out the contours of our faces. It would not do to let him really see our eyes. Hence the white robes.

Earl Marshal may be startled, but he is too old a hand at the uncanny and the unusual to do more than blanch. Even as a child he was able to disguise his fears, joking with King Stephen's hangmen when they threatened him. Or perhaps he is now too weak to respond. He waits until the cloth is laid and the soup bowl with the mushrooms and bread set before him. He waits until the cipher Basset leaves the room again, for only d'Erley will he allow to feed him, to see him in his ultimate weakness. It is d'Erley, alone, who wipes his bowels and changes the towels kept between his legs to stanch the flow which he can no longer control.

Basset leaves and the earl turns his head slightly, speaking in a whisper to d'Erley, who must put his head down next to the old man's mouth in order to hear. The earl does this for a reason, knowing how much d'Erley is comforted and discomforted by the closeness of their connection. However, he does not realize that his breath stinks, a compote of age and decay. If he did, it would discomfort *him*, for he was ever a meticulous man.

But d'Erley, blinkered, can see nothing but the old man's covers, the red cross, the plate.

"Do you see what I see?" Marshal asks. Since d'Erley does not at first understand him, the earl is forced to repeat it twice more, weakening with each word.

"My Lord, I do not know what that might be," d'Erley says, sure it is Death the earl sees, has seen these past two months. But he is early in his assessment by days. My brother is busy elsewhere, reaping still in the sands around Jerusalem and in the deltas of Africa, in London's awful slums.

"By my soul," the earl says, the confession strong in his mouth, the very word exciting us to a fresh brilliance, "I see two men in white, one is beside me on the right, the other on the left. Nowhere have I seen men so fine."

Having been properly observed, we allow ourselves to fade away. Not men, of course. There are but three of us in all the universe, and though I say "brother" it is but a convenience, a nod to the sexing of language in this world. We wear no gender. We do not reproduce. We are three and we are one, together, forever.

But the earl, though he has seen us, he sees us as he would have us, not as we are. Besides, in his old age he has developed problems with his vision, seeing rather less well than did his father, who lost an eye at the convent of Wherewhell when the melting lead of a fired roof dripped directly upon his face. We were neither to the earl's left nor his right, but rather hovering over his great bed.

But he had seen what he was meant to see, what the history says he saw. Witnessing, he passes it on, impressing it upon d'Erley, whose memory will serve as the maker of the *chanson*. Thus is the loop of history preserved.

D'Erley answers, "My Lord, thus there come to you a company that will lead you in the true way," neglecting to ask for more details from the man he worships, loves, fears. It is just as well. Details would only serve to confuse. Only the angels of Revelations have eyes all around and within, in front and behind. D'Erley will task himself with this neglect for years to come, and that, too, will go into his history.

So we pass from the scene, my brother and I, through the thick stone walls of Caversham, over the lead roof, into the darkening night sky where a single moon lends its feeble light.

We give little thought to our other brother, who will pass this way a few days hence only to discover how meager are our leavings. They will be rinsed well with rose water, stiffening in a chamber already stripped of its possessions by the earl himself, giving away his gowns and gold for the good of a soul which he no longer owns. Yet he has us to thank for so quiet and peaceful an end. It is only the ones we cannot find loving history for who die in agony, like Marshal's first master, Henry Plantagenet, devoured by the disease that first seized him by the heel. He was forced by our brother to drag himself around his rooms like some poor, miserable beast, moaning until the end when the clotted blood fell from his mouth and nose and he lay quite alone.

We never dwell on our failures or our brother's successes. In truth we do not understand them. None of us recalls the beginning, only this endless circuit, this cosmic encircling, this treadmill of souls. Each year we discover another song, another story brought down through the ages that smells of truth, and ride its memory back through the years, though we have been confused more than once. Humans are consummate actors in the camera's eye. Sometimes it is a true memory and then we do feast. More often there is a false trail, and then there is famine.

Perhaps some day we will even claim Henry Plantagenet's soul, finding a history left by Eleanor, who once loved him, though certainly his sons did not. Then we could bring his dying a little peace. He might even rest his last days in a bed, brought mushrooms and wine by a beloved counselor, and we would shine on him with our white robes. Or, if he preferred, halos and harps; we could provide those.

But that is another *perhaps* and foolish of me to maunder so. Besides, we are planning our next besiegement, for a scholar has recently discovered an account of the life and death of

Arthur's only son, written by the one who loved him, his devouring mother, the Fey. There are only twenty-seven parchment leaves, written in a strange Gaelic, and two leaves are missing. But each leaf contains two columns of forty lines. If it is true, it promises to be quite a feast. And in our turn, we promise to give him a quiet, soulless ending.

Selah.

So there I was, sitting in Buckley Recital Hall at Amherst College, listening to Silly Wizard chew the musical scenery, when the band played a tune called "The Nine Points of Roguery." Well, I could only think of five myself — and got no help from the band with their impenetrable Scots accents. Using the music as background, I scribbled the opening paragraphs on my program and finished the story the following week.

The Five Points of Roguery

The land of Dun D'Addin is known for its rogues, though how so many could have been crowded into so small and homey a place has never been explained. Dun D'Addin is really only one great hill, a land cast off from its neighbors by its height. Folks there live On-the-Hill, By-the-Hill, Over-the-Hill, and ones still on the run from the law live Under-the-Hill, and it gives them all a rather lumpish disposition.

There are no main streets, only rough paths most often laced with vines: thornbush and prickleweed and the rough-toothed caught-ums. The trees tend to grow sideways away from the hill, dropping the wrinkled and bitter fruit into the borderlands.

Dun D'Addin is a place meant to be passed over or passed through or passed by on the way to somewhere else, and that is why there is only the one inn, atop the hill, called — perversely — the Bird and the Babe, though it has little to do with either. It is in that inn, before the great central hearth, that the hill's resident rogues gather and try to outwit one another with their boasting tales. They are rather pathetically proud of their reputation for roguery, but it is really only of the smash-and-grab variety. True finesse is, I am afraid, quite beyond them — as they found out one evening in front of the fire at the Bird and the Babe, to their eternal chagrin and everlasting regret.

"There was an old fiddling tune called 'Nine Points of Roguery' in the land I came from," said Sly-fingered Jok. "But of course that's absurd."

"Why?" asked the Innkeeper. He knew his role in these discussions. He had a positive genius for keeping conversation, especially brag-tales, flowing. That genius consisted mainly of asking one-word questions at the right time.

"Why? Because I can only think of five," said Jok. "And you have to agree that I am about as roguish a fellow as you are likely to meet in the highways and byways of Dun D'Addin."

The men at the hearthfire chuckled, each of them silently thinking himself the greater rogue. And besides, Dun D'Addin's highways were crackled with grass, and the byways ruts of mud both in and out of the rainy season.

Innkeeper used his silence to bless Jok. Chuckling men are drinking men, was his thought. He made his money without roguery but by supplying vast quantities of ale to the listeners and supplying to travelers a few straw pallets and a thin blanket for the night.

One florid fat man, a stranger and obviously a merchant by his garb, put up his finger. It was missing the top knuckle. The bottom two signed grotesquely at the Innkeeper. "Drinks around," said the merchant. "I want to hear about these five points of roguery, especially from the mouth of a rogue."

"Point one," said Jok, smiling and then sipping on his ale, "is the Eye." He winked at them all and they gave him a laugh.

"Eye?" asked the Innkeeper, right in rhythm.

"The Eye," said Jok. "It must be clear and bright and honest-seeming, and never a wink between you and your Pick." Then he winked again, more broadly this time, and laughed with them.

The listeners settled back in their chairs. The fat man

grunted as fat men will, rooting around in his chair like a pig in wallow, but at last he, too, was ready. Jok, staring at him openly, patiently, waited to begin.

One: The Eye

There was a man, a constant traveler and purveyor of goods not quite his own, if you take my meaning (said Jok), who through a great misfortune had been maimed in the war. But he turned this to his own profit, as you will see. A man who can do that could be king, though his kingdom be no more than a cherrystone and his people only ants.

(Though his kingdom be no more than a muddy hill, said the fat man under his breath, and his people no more than rogues.)

He had, in his travels, acquired a diamond the size of a knuckle, and its original owner, the local high sheriff, was not pleased at its disappearance. The borders of the land were sealed, and at every turning, armed men were posted in pairs to search travelers — and one another — to find the precious jewel.

In the course of their searchings, they had uncovered many a thief and villain, and the trees along the borderlands were festooned with bodies, since thievery was rewarded with hanging in those times. It was a heavy harvest.

But that did not worry our traveler. He boldly stepped up the line and had himself searched. With a steady eye, he winked at one soldier and let them rip through the innocent seams of his coat. They even cored his apple and examined the pips. He thanked them for preparing his meal and waved as he walked through the orchard of ripe souls. He was careful not to run.

And when he got to the other side of the dark wood, where Dun D'Addin's hill began, he smiled. The he popped out the staring false eye into his hand; the real one had been put out in war. He winkled the diamond from his eye socket and, whistling, went to sell the jewel at an eye-catching price to the Fence-Who-Lives-On-The-Hill.

"Did he really?" asked the Innkeeper, forced to use three words instead of one but still sure of the bargain.

"I knew a man with a blind eye once, but never a socket that could glitter like that," said a listener. "And I've lived in Dun D'Addin all my life, high on it, as they say." He slapped his thigh. He was a storekeeper by trade and a gambler by inclination and thus poor at both.

Jok smiled at the storekeeper, at the Innkeeper, at the fat man a-wallow in the chair, and then at his newly filled glass, but did not answer. Instead, he took a sip of his drink.

"That was a bit of a joke rather than a pointer," said the florid fat man. "I expected more." He signed again with his mutilated hand.

"Wounded in the war, sir?" asked Jok at last, staring at the hand without flinching.

"No," said the fat man. "Caught it in my uncle's till when I was but a boy. I've learned a lot since." He smiled. "But I've come up on the hill, to the home of more prosperous thieves, to learn more. So — what is your second point of roguery?"

Jok stared at the grotesque hand with the puckered knuckle in place of a nail. "Point two — the Hand," he said. "Fast and mobile and quicker than the eye."

"Quicker than a fake eye?" called out a listener, a miller who had given false weight and been driven out of his town before settling atop Dun D'Addin's hill.

They all chuckled, ready to listen again.

Two: The Hand

There was a surgeon's apprentice (continued Jok) who lined his pockets with the buying and selling of body parts. Hanged murderers, suicides buried at crossroads, and the pickings after battle were his stock-in-trade. He did not traffic in the appendages of steady husbands and faithful wives, but had a rather brisk business along the border of Dun D'Addin with the sawed-off limbs of felons, miscreants, and malefactors.

Who bought these parts? For the most, it was alchemists and devil worshippers, trespassers in the forbidden zone. I do not think he asked, nor would they have answered him. What he did not know could not hurt, was his motto. His was a grisly but profitable trade.

It happened late one night, when he was applying his singular skill and saw to the body of the late and unlamented Strangler of Hareton Heath, a corpse that had one leg shorter than the other because — it was said — he had lived so long on Dun D'Addin's hill, that there came a loud knock on the door, a veritable drum roll of knuckles.

Startled, the surgeon's apprentice cried out.

"Who is there?" His voice was an agony of squeaks.

"Open in the name of the king's own law," came the call.

It was, of course, too late to hide the evidence of his night's work, for that was spilled all about him. And there was no denying his part in it. Evisceration is a messy business; it leaves its own bloody calling cards. Gathering his wits about him — and leaving the late Strangler's on the table — he donned his black coat and black hat, a midnight disguise,

Just as he slipped out the back door, the king's law broke down the front.

The lead dragoon spotted the hand of the surgeon's apprentice still on the doorknob. Grabbing onto the hand, the dragoon cried out, "Sir, I have him."

That, of course, is when the hand came off in his, for it was the Strangler's hand, hard and horned from its horrible vocation. The apprentice had carried it off with him for just such an emergency.

The soldier, being an honest sort, screamed and dropped the severed claw. In the ensuing melee, the apprentice escaped. It is said he climbed Dun D'Addin in a single breath and was on the far side before he thought to stay. And here he has plied a similar trade — but that is only a rumor, and not one that I, at least, can vouch for.

"I'll give you a hand for that tale," cried out a lusty listener, the local butcher, clapping loudly but alone.

Jok smiled and bowed his head toward the applause. "So point two is the Hand."

The fat man sighed. "And I expected more from you than yet another joke. I suppose point three is the same?" He scratched under his eye with the mutilated finger.

Jok, fascinated, could not stop staring at him. "No," he said at last. "As a matter of fact, point three is *very* serious."

"Three!" said the Innkeeper, suddenly remembering his role in the affair. "Three!"

"Point three," Jok said, tearing his gaze from the fat man and looking again at his audience, which had enlarged by four or five drinkers, much to the Innkeeper's satisfaction. "Point three is the Voice. In roguery, that voice must be melodic and cozening but, in the end, forgettable."

Three: The Voice

Ellyne was the fairest girl on any of Dun D'Addin's borders, the fairest in seven counties, if one were to be exact. Her hair was red and curled about her face like little fishhooks ready to catch the unwary ogler. Her skin was the color of berried cream, rosy and white. Not a man but sighed for her, though she seemed oblivious to them all.

One day she was walking out in the woods, not far from the hill, picking bellflowers for a tisane and listening to the syncopations of the birds, when a rogue from Dun D'Addin chanced by.

Now his name was Vyctor, and he was known Under-the-Hill as The Voice, for he could cast the sound of it where he willed. It was his one great trick, that mellifluous traveling tone. With it he had talked jewelers out of their gems, good wives out of their virtue, and a judge out of hanging him. He was *that* good.

Vyctor saw the redheaded Ellyne and was stunned, felled, split, and spitted by her beauty. He had heard tell of it, but that had been on Dun D'Addin's byways, where every word is doubled and every truth halved. But those who had praised Ellyne's beauty hadn't sung the smallest part of it properly. Vyctor the Voice lost his — and his heart as well. He began to stammer.

Now Ellyne was used to the stammering of men. In fact, she was of the belief that — except for her own father and a blind singer in her town — all men above the age of puberty stammered. She was an innocent for sure, and not aware of her beauty, for not a man had been able to string three words together to tell her of it.

But if Vyctor could not speak directly to her, he could still talk by throwing his voice, and so he spoke to her from the nearest tree.

"Beauteous maid," the birch began.

Ellyne turned round and about, the movement making her hair a halo and bringing a magnificent flush to her cheek. For a moment even the birch stammered; then it went on.

"Beauteous maid, you make my sap run fast; you make my bark tingle. I would embrace you."

Well, Ellyne had never heard a tree talk before, and she was fascinated. It was so well spoken, and besides, it was giving her compliments instead of the stuttering and spitting and gawking she was used to from all the men of her acquaintance. She moved closer to hear more.

Vyctor took a step or two in the tree's direction, and the birch continued its serenade.

"My love for you is deeply rooted," said the birch. "Do not ever leaf me."

Ellyne sighed.

Just then the wind came up and blew the birch branches about. One grazed Ellyne's arm. She shrieked — for she was a good girl and not about to be touched before the wedding banns had been posted.

Vyctor leaned forward, his sword suddenly in hand. "I...I...I will save you," he cried, forgetting for that instant that the birch was his spokes-tree. He lay about vigorously and had soon carved up enough firewood to keep the hearths of Dun D'Addin warm for a week.

"Monster!" cried Ellyne. "You have slain my own tree love." She fell upon the woodpile and wept.

From the back she was not as beautiful as the front, and Vyctor came immediately to his senses. Besides, her noisy sobbing had alerted the local dragoons, all of whom were in love with her, and a company of them marched into the woods, bayonets fixed.

Vyctor was arrested and tried, but his Voice having made a full recovery, he was released.

Ellyne carried half a dozen of the finest birch branches home and placed them tenderly over her mantel. Then she took the surname Tree. She was careful not to burn wood or eat vegetables thereafter, and wore widow's weed the rest of her life.

The laughter that greeted Jok's third tale signaled another round of ale. Innkeeper was just pouring, when the miller said, "If that's three, what's four?"

Jok smiled. "Eye, Hand, Voice," he said slowly, ticking them off on the fingers of his left hand. "But the fourth point of roguery is…"

"*The Great Escape!*" came a voice floating back from outside. Then the door snicked shut.

"The Great Escape," Jok agreed. "Now there was a rogue…"

"My purse!" cried the man closest to the fire. "It's been cut!"

Jok turned white and held his hands out in front of him, staring as honestly as he could at the accusing man. "I am not the culprit, sir. Look. I am clean. I stand here empty." He turned out his pockets.

Every man in the inn, used to the ways of Dun D'Addin, did the same.

Innkeeper came to the center of the circle of men and looked around. Someone was missing. It was the fat, florid merchant with the maimed hand. He was gone. And *all* their purses were gone as well.

Of course Slip-fingered Jok never told this final part of the tale. Even if he had known it, it would not have helped his reputation as a rogue. But in a nearby land, in a larger inn, known perversely as the Eagle

*and the Child, though it had nothing to do with either, a rather florid
thin man, lying back on the very pillows that had lent him substance,
told this tale to me, naming the points of roguery on his fingers. But
he lacked one finger, and therein lay his own miscalculation, for I
relieved him of his pants and purse when he thought to make a long
and interesting night. And so I end the tale. For the first three points
of roguery may be Eye and Hand and Voice, and the fourth the
Great Escape. But the fifth and final point, which every true rogue
knows well, is the Last Laugh. And I have often been complimented
on the engaging quality of mine.*

My father, a publicity and public relations exec, had a creative memory. My mother wrote short stories and created and sold double crostics and crossword puzzles. My brother is a journalist and desktop publisher in Brazil. Our family has always drowned in stories. Annie was a live-in nurse/nanny/mother's helper, a big, blowsy Irish woman, who used to take me to church on Sundays. That I was Jewish didn't stop her. She was also a closet anti-Semite, which came out a long time after, but — as she exclaimed to my mother — she didn't mean "little Janie." And she didn't.

Family Stories

My father's stories
were tightly held.
He was stingy
with the past,
coining what
he would not remember,
parceling out the rest
with the cautious philanthropy
of a miser.
His lips moved
with the effort.

My mother's stories
waterfalled out
in little spurts
between apologies.
They were all praises,
Sunday school tales,
the morals
spoken in italics
so we could not miss the points.

But we would not miss
the tellings.

Our old nurse Annie
had no tales of her own,
only the ones
she had heard
and she had heard
and she had heard before.
She was not born
but made whole
to tell us stories.
Her past was one
filled with gods
and mothers-of-gods
and the little imp tales
that we loved the best.

My brother and I
are pieced together
like crazy quilts.
We keep warm
on winter evenings
with the weight
of all those tales.
But we never tell them
to one another.
We can't recall them,
only the ones that begin
"Do you remember when…
Do you remember?"

MERLE
INSINGA
1991

The first few paragraphs of this came to me when I was on a ten-day author tour of Fairbanks, Alaska. It has absolutely nothing to do with Alaska in March except that the young woman from the Arts Council who was my spirit guide showed me an angel story she wrote, a sensational piece. It made me open to angels. I wrote those paragraphs on a borrowed typewriter in my host's home in between gigs. I expected mammoth amounts of you-are-a-Satanist letters to flood the magazine after its publication. There were none. Go figure.

An Infestation of Angels

The angels came again today, filthy things, dropping golden-hard wing feathers and turds as big and brown as camel dung. This time one of them took Isak, clamping him from behind with massive talons. We could hear him screaming long after the covey was out of sight. His blood stained the doorpost where they took him. We left it there, part warning, part desperate memorial, with the dropped feathers nailed above. In a time of plagues, this infestation of angels was the worst.

We did not want to stay in the land of the Gipts, but slaves must do as their masters command. And though we were not slaves in the traditional sense, only hirelings, we had signed contracts and the Gipts are great believers in contracts. It was a saying of theirs that "One who goes back on his signed word is no better than a thief." What they do to thieves is considered grotesque even in this godforsaken desert-land.

So we were trapped here, under skies that rained frogs, amid sparse fields that bred locusts, beneath a sun that raised rashes and blisters on our sensitive skins. It was a year of unnature. Yet if any one of us complained, the leader of the Gipts, the faró, waved the contract high over his head, causing his followers to break into that high ululation they mis-call laughter.

We stayed.

Minutes after Isak was taken, his daughter Miriamne came to my house with the Rod of Leaders. I carved my own sign below Isak's and then spoke the solemn oath in our ancient tongue to Miriamne and the nine others who came to witness the passing of the stick. My sign was a snake, for my clan is Serpent. It had been exactly twelve rotations since the last member of Serpent had led the People here, but if the plague of angels lasted much longer, there would be no one else of my tribe to carry on in this place. We were not a warrior clan and I was the last. We had always been a small clan, and poor, ground under the heels of the more prosperous tribes.

When the oath was done and properly attested to — we are a people of parchment and ink — we sat down at the table together to break bread.

"We cannot stay longer," began Josu. His big, bearded face was so crisscrossed with scars it looked like a map, and the southern hemisphere was moving angrily. "We must ask the faró to let us out of our contract."

"In all the years of our dealings with the Gipts," I pointed out, "there has never been a broken contract. My father and yours, Josu, would turn in their graves knowing we even consider such a thing." My father, comfortably dead these fifteen years back in the Homeland, would not have bothered turning, no matter what the cause. But Josu's father, like all those of Scorpion, had been the anxious type, always looking for extra trouble. It took little imagination to picture him rotating in the earth like a lamb on a holiday spit.

Miriamne wept silently in the corner, but her brothers pounded the table with fists as broad as hammers.

"He *must* let us go!" Ur shouted.

"Or at least," his younger, larger brother added sensibly, "he must let us put off the work on his temple until the angels migrate north. It is almost summer."

Miriamne was weeping aloud now, though whether for Isak's sudden bloody death or at the thought of his killers in the lush high valleys of the north was difficult to say.

"It will do us no good to ask the faró to let us go," I said. "For if we do, he will use us as the Gipts always use thieves, and that is not a happy prospect." By *us*, of course, I meant me, for the faró's wrath would be visited upon the asker, which, as leader, would be me. "But…" I paused, pauses being the coin of Serpent's wisdom.

They looked expectant.

"…if we could persuade the faró that this plague was meant for the Gipts and not us…" I left that thought in front of them. The Serpent clan is known for its deviousness and wit, and deviousness and wit were what was needed now, in this time of troubles.

Miriamne stopped weeping. She walked around the table and stood behind me, putting her hands on my shoulders.

"I stand behind Masha," she said.

"And I." It was Ur, who always followed his sister's lead.

And so, one by one by one, the rest of the minon agreed. What the ten agreed to, the rest of the People in the land of the Gipts would do without question. In this loyalty lay our strength.

I went at once to the great palace of the faró, for if I waited much longer he would not understand the urgency of my mission. The Gipts are a fat race with little memory, which is why they have others build them large reminders. The deserts around are littered with their monuments — stone and bone and mortar tokens cemented with the People's blood. Ordinarily we do not complain of this. After all, we are the only ones who can satisfactorily plan and construct these mammoth memories.

The Gipts are incapable on their own. Instead they squat upon their vast store of treasures, doling out golden tokens for work. It is a strange understanding we have, but no stranger than some of nature's other associations. Does not the sharp-beaked plover feed upon the crocodile's back? Does not the tiny remora cling to the shark?

But this year the conditions in the Gipt kingdom had been intolerable. While we often lose a few of the People to the heat, to the badly-prepared Giptanese food, or to the ever-surprising visit of the Gipt pox, there had never before been such a year: plague after plague after plague. There were dark murmurs everywhere that our God had somehow been angered. And the last, this hideous infestation.

Normally angels stay within their mountain fasts, feasting on wild goats and occasional nestlings. They are rarely seen, except from afar on their spiraling mating flights when the males circle the heavens, caroling and displaying their stiffened pinions and erections to their females who watch from the heights. (There are, of course, stories of Gipt women who, inflamed by the sight of that strange, winged masculinity, run off into the wilds and are never seen again. Women of the People would never do such a thing.)

However, this year there had been a severe drought and the mountain foliage was sparse. Many goats died of starvation. The angels, hungry for red meat, had found our veins carried the same sweet nectar. Working out on the monuments, walking along the streets unprotected, we were easier prey than the horned goats. And the Gipts allow us to carry no weapons. It is in the contract.

Fifty-seven had fallen to the angel claws, ten of them of my own precious clan. It was too many. We had to convince the faró that this plague was his problem and not ours. It would take all of the deviousness and wit of a true Serpent. I thought quickly as I walked down the great wide street, the Street of Memories, towards the palace of the faró.

Because the Gipts think a woman's face and ankle can cause unnecessary desire, both had to be suitably draped. I wore the traditional black robe and pants that covered my legs, and the black silk mask that hid all but my eyes. However, a builder needs to be able to move easily, and it was hot in this land, so my stomach and arms were bare. Those parts of the body were considered undistinguished by the Gipts. It occurred to me as I walked that my stomach and arms were thereby flashing unmistakable signals to any angels on the prowl. My grip on the Rod of Leadership tightened. I shifted to carry it between both hands. I would not go meekly, as Isak had, clamped from behind. I twirled and looked around, then glanced up and scanned the skies.

There was nothing there but the clear, untrammeled blue of the Gipt summer canopy. Not even a bird wrote in lazy script across that slate.

And so I got to the palace without incident. The streets had been as bare as the sky. Normally the streets would be a-squall with the People and other hirelings of the Gipts. *They* only traveled in donkey-drawn chairs and at night, when their overweight, ill-proportioned bodies can stand the heat. And since the angels are a diurnal race, bedding down in their aeries at night, Gipts and angels rarely meet.

I knocked at the palace door. The guards, mercenaries hired from across the great water, their black faces mapped with ritual scars, opened the doors from within. I nodded slightly. In the ranks of the Gipts, the People were higher than they. However, it says in our holy books that all shall be equal, so I nodded.

They did not return my greetings. Their own religion counted mercenaries as dead men until they came back home.

The dead do not worry about the niceties of conversation.

"Masha-la, Masha-la," came a twittering cry.

I looked up and saw the faró's twenty sons bearing down on me, their foreshortened legs churning along the hall. Still too young to have gained the enormous weight that marked their elders, the boys climbed upon me like little monkeys. I was a great favorite at court, using my Serpent's wit to construct wonder tales for their entertainment.

"Masha-la, tell us a story:"

I held out the Rod and they fell back, astonished to see it in my hand. It put an end to our casual story sessions. "I must see your father, the great faró," I said.

They raced back down the hall, chittering and smacking their lips as the smell of the food in the dining commons drew them in. I followed, knowing that the adult Gipts would be there as well, partaking of one of their day-long feasts.

Two more black mercenaries opened the doors for me. Of a different tribe, these were tall and thin, the scarifications on their arms like jeweled bracelets of black beads. I nodded to them in passing. Their faces reflected nothing back.

The hall was full of feeding Gipts, served by their slimmer women. On the next to highest tier, there was a line of couches on which lay seven massive men, the faró's advisors. And on the high platform, overseeing them all, the mass of flesh that was the faró himself, one fat hand reaching towards a bowl of peeled grapes.

"Greetings, oh high and mighty faró," I said, my voice rising above the sounds in the hall.

The faró smiled blandly and waved a lethargic hand. The rings on his fingers bit deeply into the engorged flesh. It is a joke amongst the People that one can tell the age of a Gipt as one does a tree, by counting the rings. Once put on, the rings become embedded by the encroaching fat. The many gems on the faró's hand winked at me. He was very old.

"Masha-la," he spoke languidly, "it grieves me to see you with the Rod of your people."

"It grieves me even more, mighty faró, to greet you with my news. But it is something which you must know." I projected my voice so that even the women in the kitchens could hear.

"Say on," said the faró.

"These death-bearing angels are not so much a plague upon the People but are rather using us as an appetizer for Giptanese flesh," I said. "Soon they will tire of our poor, ribby meat and gorge themselves on yours. Unless…" I paused.

"Unless what, *Leader of the People?*" asked the faró.

I was in trouble. Still, I had to go on. There was no turning back, and this the faró knew. "Unless my people take a small vacation across the great sea, returning when the angels are gone. We will bring more of the People and the monument will be done on time."

The faró's greedy eyes glittered. "For no more than the promised amount?"

"It is for your own good," I whined. The faró expects petitioners to whine. It is in the contract under "Deportment Rules."

"I do not believe you, Masha-la," said the faró. "But you tell a good story. Come back tomorrow."

That saved my own skin, but it did not help the rest. "These angels *will* be after the sons of the faró," I said. It was a guess. Only the sons and occasional and unnecessary women still went out in the daylight. I am not sure why I said it. "And once they have tasted Gipt flesh…" I paused.

There was a sudden and very real silence in the room. It was clear I had overstepped myself. It was clearer when the faró sat up. Slowly that mammoth body raised with the help of two of the black guards. When he was seated upright, he put on his helm of office, with the decorated flaps that draped against his ears. He held out his hand and the guard on the right pushed the Great Gipt Crook into his pudgy palm.

"You and your People will not go to the sea this year before time," intoned the faró. "But tomorrow *you* will come to the kitchen and serve up your hand for my soup."

He banged the crook's wide bottom on the floor three times. The guard took the crook from his hand. Then exhausted by the sentence he had passed on my hand — I hoped they would take the left, not the right — he lay down again and started to eat.

I walked out, through doors opened by the shadow men, whose faces I forgot as soon as I saw them, out into the early eve, made blood red by the setting sun.

I could hear the patter of the faró's sons after me, but such was my agitation that I did not turn to warn them back. Instead I walked down the street composing a psalm to the cunning of my right hand, just in case.

The chittering of the boys behind me increased and, just as I came to the door of Isak's house, I turned and felt the weight of wind from above. I looked up and saw an angel swooping down on me, wings fast to its side in a perilous stoop like a hawk upon its prey. I fell back against the doorpost, reaching my right hand up in supplication. My fingers scraped against the nailed-up feathers. Instinctively I grabbed them and held them clenched in my fist. My left hand was down behind me scrabbling in the dirt. It mashed something on the ground. And then the angel was on me and my left hand joined the right pushing up against the awful thing.

Angel claws were inches from my neck when something stopped the creature's rush. Its wings whipped out and slowed its descent, and its great golden-haired head moved from side to side.

It was then that I noticed its eyes. They were as blue as the Gipt sky — and as empty. The angel lifted its beautiful blank face upward and sniffed the air, pausing curiously several times at my outstretched hands. Then, pumping its mighty wings twice, it lifted away from me, banked sharply to the right, and took off in the direction of the palace, where the faró's sons scattered before it like twigs in the wind.

Two times the angel dropped down and came up with a child in its claw. I leaped to my feet, smeared the top of my stick with dung and feathers and chased after the beast, but I was too late. It was gone, a screaming boy in each talon, heading towards its aerie, where it would share its catch.

What could I tell the faró that he would not already know from the hysterical children ahead of me? I walked back to my own house, carrying my stick above my head. It would protect me as no totem had before. I knew now what only dead men had known, the learning which they had gathered as the claws carried them above the earth! *Angels are blind and hunt by smell.* If we but smeared our sticks with their dung and feathers and carried this above our heads, we would be safe; we would be, in their "eyes," angels.

I washed my hands carefully, called the minon to me, and told them of my plan. We would go this night, as a people, to the faró. We would tell him that his people were cursed by our God now. The angels would come for them, but not for us. He would have to let us go.

It was the children's story that convinced him, as mine could not. Luck had it that the two boys taken were his eldest. Or perhaps not luck. As they were older, they were fatter — and slower. The angel came upon them first.

Their flesh must have been sweet. In the morning we could hear the hover of angel wings outside, like a vast buzzing. Some of the People wanted to sneak away by night.

"No," I commanded, holding up the Rod of Leadership, somewhat darkened by the angel dung smeared over the top. "If we sneak away like thieves in the night, we will never work for the Gipts again. We must go tomorrow morning, in the light of day, through the cloud of angels. That way the faró and his people will know our power and the power of our God."

"But," said Josu, "how can we be sure your plan will work? It is a devious one at best. I am not sure even I believe you."

"Watch!" I said and I opened the door, holding the Rod over my head. I hoped that what I believed to be so was so, but my heart felt like a marble in the mouth.

The door slammed behind me and I knew faces pressed against the curtains of each window.

And then I was alone in the courtyard, armed with but a stick and a prayer.

The moment I walked outside, the hover of angels became agitated. They spiraled up and, like a line of enormous insects, winged towards me. As they approached, I prayed and put the stick above my head.

The angels formed a great circle high over my head and one by one they dipped down, sniffed around the top of the Rod, then flew back to place. When they were satisfied, they wheeled off, flying in a phalanx, towards the farthest hills.

At that, the doors of the houses opened, and the People emerged. Josu was first, his own stick, sticky with angel dung, in hand.

"Now, quick," I said, "before the faró can see what we are doing, grab up what dung and feathers you find from that circle and smear it quickly on the doorposts of the houses. Later, when we are sure no one is watching, we can scrape it onto totems to carry with us to the sea."

And so it was done. The very next morning, with much

blowing of horns and beating of drums, we left for the sea. But none of the faró's people or his mercenaries came to see us off, though they followed us later.

But that is another story altogether, and not a pretty tale at all.

Ann Jordan asked for a story about home towns for her anthology Fires of the Past. *I obliged, combining the quiet — almost comatose — atmosphere of Hatfield, Massachusetts, where I have lived the past twenty years, with the twelve-year-ago invasion of Great Gray owls which so fascinated our bird-watching family, especially my husband David and our youngest son Jason. Also, I have always wanted to write a mystery story,* à la *Ruth Rendell* .

Great Gray

The cold spike of winter wind struck Donnal full in the face as he pedaled down River Road toward the marsh. He reveled in the cold just as he reveled in the ache of his hands in the wool gloves and the pull of muscle along the inside of his right thigh.

At the edge of the marsh, he got off the bike, tucking it against the sumac, and crossed the road to the big field. He was lucky this time. One of the Great Grays, the larger of the two, was perched on a tree. Donnal lifted the field glasses to his eyes and watched as the bird, undisturbed by his movement, regarded the field with its big yellow eyes.

Donnal didn't know a great deal about birds, but the newspapers had been full of the *invasion*, as it was called. Evidently Great Gray owls were Arctic birds that only every hundred years found their way in large numbers to towns as far south as Hatfield. He shivered, as if a Massachusetts town on the edge of the Berkshires was south. The red-back vole population in the north had crashed and the young Great Grays had fled their own hunger and the talons of the older birds. And here they were, daytime owls, fattening themselves on the mice and voles common even in winter in Hatfield.

Donnal smiled, and watched the bird as it took off, spreading its six-foot wings and sailing silently over the field. He knew there were other Great Grays in the Valley — two in Amherst, one in the Northampton Meadows, three reported in Holyoke, and some twenty others between Hatfield and Boston. But he felt that the two in Hatfield were his alone. So far no one else had discovered them. He had been biking out twice a day for over a week to watch them, a short three miles along the meandering road.

A vegetarian himself, even before he'd joined the Metallica commune in Turner's Falls, Donnal had developed an unnatural desire to watch animals feeding, as if that satisfied any of his dormant carnivorous instincts. He'd even owned a boa at one time, purchasing white mice for it at regular intervals. It was one of the reasons he'd been asked to leave the commune. The other, hardly worth mentioning, had more to do with a certain sexual ambivalence having to do with children. Donnal never thought about *those* things anymore. But watching the owls feeding made him aware of how much superior he was to the hunger of mere beasts.

"It makes me understand what is meant by a little lower than the angels," he'd remarked to his massage teacher that morning, thinking about angels with great gray wings.

This time the owl suddenly plummeted down, pouncing on something which it carried in its talons as it flew back to the tree. Watching through the field glasses, Donnal saw it had a mouse. He shivered deliciously as the owl plucked at the mouse's neck, snapping the tiny spinal column. Even though he was much too far away to hear anything, Donnal fancied a tiny dying shriek and the satisfying s*nick* as the beak crunched through bone. He held his breath in three great gasps as the owl swallowed the mouse whole. The last thing Donnal saw was the mouse's tail stuck for a moment out of the beak like a piece of gray velvet spaghetti.

Afterward, when the owl flew off, Donnal left the edge of the field and picked his way across the crisp snow to the tree. Just as he hoped, the pellet was on the ground by the roots.

Squatting, the back of his neck prickling with excitement, Donnal took off his gloves and picked up the pellet. For a minute he just held it in his right hand, wondering at how light and how dry the whole thing felt. Then he picked it apart. The mouse's skull was still intact, surrounded by bits of fur. Reaching into the pocket of his parka, Donnal brought out the silk scarf he'd bought a week ago at the Mercantile just for this purpose. The scarf was blood red with little flecks of dark blue. He wrapped the skull carefully in the silk and slipped the packet into his pocket, then turned a moment to survey the field again. Neither of the owls was in sight.

Patting the pocket thoughtfully, he drew his gloves back on and strode back toward his bike. The wind had risen and snow was beginning to fall. He let the wind push him along as he rode, almost effortlessly, back to the center of town.

Donnal had a room in a converted barn about a quarter of a mile south of the center. The room was within easy walking to his massage classes and only about an hour's bike ride into Northampton, even closer to the grocery store. His room was dark and low and had a damp, musty smell as if it still held the memory of cows and hay in its beams. Three other families shared the main part of the barn, ex-hippies like Donnal, but none of them from the commune. He had found the place by biking through each of the small Valley towns, their names like some sort of English poem: Hadley, Whately, Sunderland, Deerfield, Heath, Goshen, Rowe. Hatfield, on the flat, was outlined by the Connecticut River on its eastern flank. There had been acres of potatoes, their white flowers waving in the breeze, when he first cycled through. He took it as an omen and when he found that the center had everything he would need — a pizza parlor, a bank, a convenience store, and a video store — had made up his mind to stay. There was a notice about the room for rent tacked up in the convenience store. He went right over and was accepted at once.

Stashing his bike in one of the old stalls, Donnal went up the rickety backstairs to his room. His boots lined up side by side by the door, he took the red scarf carefully out of his pocket. Cradling it in two hands, he walked over to the mantel which he'd built from a long piece of wood he'd found in the back, sanding and polishing the wood by hand all summer long.

He bowed his head a moment, remembering the owl flying on its silent wings over the field, pouncing on the mouse, picking at the animal's neck until it died, then swallowing it whole. Then he smiled and unwrapped the skull.

He placed it on the mantel and stepped back, silently counting. There were seventeen little skulls there now. Twelve were mice, four were voles. One, he was sure, was a weasel's.

Lost in contemplation, he didn't hear the door open, the quick intake of breath. Only when he had finished his hundredth repetition of the mantra and turned did Donnal realize that little Jason was staring at the mantel.

"You..." Donnal began, the old rhythm of his heart spreading a heat down his back. "You are not supposed to come in without knocking, Jay. Without being..." He took a deep breath and willed the heat away. "Invited."

Jason nodded silently, his eyes still on the skulls.

"Did you hear me?" Donnal forced his voice to be soft but he couldn't help noticing that Jason's hair was as velvety as mouse skin. Donnal jammed his hands into his pockets. "Did you?"

Jason looked at him then, his dark eyes wide, vaguely

unfocused. He nodded but did not speak. He never spoke.

"Go back to your apartment," Donnal said, walking the boy to the door. He motioned with his head, not daring to remove his hands from his pockets. "Now."

Jason disappeared through the door and Donnal shut it carefully with one shoulder, then leaned against it. After a moment, he drew his hands out of his pockets. They were trembling and moist.

He stared across the room at the skulls. They seemed to glow, but it was only a trick of the light, nothing more.

Donnal lay down on his futon and thought about nothing but the owls until he fell asleep. It was dinner time when he finally woke. As he ate he thought — and not for the first time — how hard winter was on vegetarians.

"But owls don't have that problem," he whispered aloud.

His teeth crunched through the celery with the same sort of *snick-snack* he thought he remembered hearing when the owl had bitten into the mouse's neck.

The next morning was one of those crisp, bright, clear winter mornings with the sun reflecting off the snowy fields with such an intensity that Donnal's eyes watered as he rode along River Road. By the water treatment building, he stopped and watched a cardinal flicking through the bare ligaments of sumac. His disability check was due and he guessed he might have a client or two as soon as he passed his exams at the Institute. He had good hands for massage and the extra money would come in handy. He giggled at the little joke: *hands... handy.* Extra money would mean he could buy the special tapes he'd been wanting. He'd use them for the accompaniment for massages and for his own meditations. Maybe even have cards made up: *Donnal McIvery, Licensed Massage Therapist,* the card would say. *Professional Massage. By Appointment Only.*

He was so busy thinking about the card, he didn't notice the car parked by the roadside until he was upon it. And it took him a minute before he realized there were three people — two men and a woman — standing on the other side of the car, staring at the far trees with binoculars.

Donnal felt hot then cold with anger. They were looking at *his* birds, *his* owls. He could see that both of the Great Grays were sitting in the eastern field, one on a dead tree down in the swampy area of the marsh and one in its favorite perch on a swamp maple. He controlled his anger and cleared his throat. Only the woman turned.

"Do you want a look?" she asked with a kind of quavering eagerness in her voice, starting to take the field glasses from around her neck.

Unable to answer, his anger still too strong, Donnal shook his head and, reaching into his pocket, took his own field glasses out. The red scarf came with it and fell to the ground. His cheeks flushed as red as the scarf as he bent to retrieve it. He knew there was no way the woman could guess what he used the scarf for, but still he felt she knew. He crumpled it tightly into a little ball and stuffed it back in his pocket. It was useless now, desecrated. He would have to use some of his disability check to buy another. He might have to miss a lesson because of it; because of *her*. Hatred for the woman flared up and it was all he could do to breathe deeply enough to force the feeling down, to calm himself. But his hands were shaking too much to raise the glasses to his eyes. When at last he could, the owls had flown, the people had gotten back into the car and driven away. Since the scarf was useless to him, he didn't even check for pellets, but got back on his bike and rode home.

Little Jason was playing outside when he got there and followed Donnal up to his room. He thought about warning the boy away again, but when he reached into his pocket and pulled out the scarf, having for the moment forgotten that the scarf's magic was lost to him, he was overcome with the red heat. He could feel great gray wings growing from his shoulders, bursting through his parka, sprouting quill, feather, vane. His mouth tasted blood. He heard the *snick-snack* of little neck bones being broken. Such a satisfying sound. When the heat abated, and his eyes cleared, he saw that the boy lay on the floor, the red scarf around his neck, pulled tight.

For a moment Donnal didn't understand. Why was Jason lying there; why was the scarf set into his neck in just that way? Then, when it came to him that his own strong hands had done it, he felt a strange satisfaction and he breathed as slowly as when he said his mantras. He laid the child out carefully on his bed and walked out of the room, closing the door behind.

He cashed the check at the local bank, then pedaled into Northampton. The Mercantile had several silk scarves, but only one red one. It was a dark red, like old blood. He bought it and folded it carefully into a little packet, then tucked it reverently into his pocket.

When he rode past the barn where he lived, he saw that there were several police cars parked in the driveway and so he didn't stop. Bending over the handlebars, he pushed with all his might, as if he could feel the stares of townsfolk.

The center was filled with cars, and two high school seniors, down from Smith Academy to buy candy, watched as he flew past. The wind at his back urged him on as he pedaled past the Main Street houses, around the meandering turns, past the treatment plant and the old barns marked with the passage of high school graffiti.

He was not surprised to see two vans by the roadside, one with out-of-state plates; he knew why they were there. Leaning his bike against one of the vans, he headed toward the swamp, his feet making crisp tracks on the crusty snow.

There were about fifteen people standing in a semicircle around the dead tree. The largest of the Great Grays sat in the crotch of the tree, staring at the circle of watchers with its yellow eyes. Slowly its head turned from left to right, eyes blinked, then another quarter turn.

The people were silent, though every once in a while one would move forward and kneel before the great bird, then as silently move back to place.

Donnal was exultant. These were not birders with field glasses and cameras. These were worshipers. Just as he was. He reached into his pocket and drew out the kerchief. Then slowly, not even feeling the cold, he took off his boots and socks, his jacket and trousers, his underpants and shirt. No one noticed him but the owl, whose yellow eyes only blinked but showed no fear.

He spoke his mantra silently and stepped closer, the scarf between his hands, moving through the circle to the foot of the tree. There he knelt, spreading the cloth to catch the pellet when it fell and baring his neck to the Great Gray's slashing beak.

MERLE
INSINGA
1991

I was asked to be Guest of Honor at the International Conference on the Fantastic in the Arts (Swanncon) in Florida, and because my daughter lived close by, I said yes. Though I was nervous about the company I was to keep, I ended up having a wonderful time with people like Brian Aldiss, Gary Wolf, and Dede Weil. We even went on a shopping expedition — too many people, too few cars. I had to sit on Charles Brown's lap (sorry, Charlie!). I had so much fun, I forgot to be nervous about giving an academic speech to a bunch of academics who all knew much more than I did about my subject. They seemed to like it anyway.

Oh, God, Here Come the Elves

Since I am a storyteller, I will begin with a story. It is a creation story, an etiological tale:

> And it came to pass in the days of the Author that she was sitting before her typewriter and contemplating a plot gone awry. Her characters, astride horses, had been riding so long, both she and they had forgotten the mission. To rectify this, she entitled the chapter "The Long Riding"[1] and, thus satisfying all, was proceeding with the tale.
>
> The characters got off their horses at last and looked about the scene. There was a grove of aspen, trembling slightly in the breeze. Around was the forest with its layers of green. And beyond the line of trees lay a great road which, only lately, they had all been endlessly riding upon.
>
> The Author paused, waiting for inspira-

tion, having settled those past weeks for perspiration instead, comforting herself with a
mantra learned from William Faulkner: "I
only write when I am inspired; fortunately I
am inspired at 9 o'clock every morning."[2]

Leaning back, the Author took a sip of tea,
waiting.

Sudden silence alerted her. The forest itself seemed to have stopped breathing. At first
there was nothing. And then — there was a
circle of some thirty mannikins, dressed all in
green jerkin and trews, as if they had meta-
morphosed from the trees and brush. Half the
size of men, with skin a greenish cast, like
translucent glaze over fine bones, as if the land
itself had been thinned down to its essence
and given human form.[3]

"Oh God," the Author groaned, putting
her hands over her eyes so as not to read the
offending words on the page. "Here come the
elves."

To understand the Author's agony, the reader must be
reminded: the book *White Jenna* is not a book about elves. It is
not a book in which little humanoid creatures of an unearthly
attenuated beauty caper about making white fire and singing in
tongues. There is but one kind of magic in White Jenna's land
and it has absolutely nothing to do with unicorns or dragons or
trolls or ents or sentient swords or philosophical bards or elves.
Especially not elves.

And yet, with an arrogance born of centuries of misrule, the
elves have casually — and without invitation — walked onto
the scene.

There are three things any author can do at this point. The first is to take a Number 2 pencil or a red or green Flair pen and declare open war on elvery. A single deadly stroke, an airborne attack, delete signs rained from above — any of these will suffice. In that way the elves and all their faery accoutrement — bells, spells, and pointed ears — will disappear from the forest as if they had never been. It will be a clean surgical strike. And if it leaves a hole — we had to destroy the novel in order to save it — at least the author will not spend days agonizing over the battle. Like the wonderfully silly song about "Railroad Bill,"[4] in which the song writer finally destroys the recalcitrant eponymous hero with his pen, the author declares the novel belongs to her and no character or characters will do other than her explicit bidding. That's number one.

There is a second course, a compromise approach. The author gives a little to the elves and takes a little away. Like most political settlements, this ends up compromising everybody. For example, the author could say: okay, the elves can stay but they are going to have to wear red rather than green. Or the author could call them Oompa-loompahs or Red Injuns or Gildensterns or Thieves' World™ Thieves. Anything but *elves*. Or the author could declare that the elves may stay for tea and leave on the 8 o'clock ferry for Lothlorien. That's number two.

The third solution, while not nearly as neat as the surgical strike nor as balanced as the compromise, is the one to which I subscribe: *total, utter, and abject surrender to the elves*.

Let me explain.

Writers are creatures of layers, an uneasy yoking of conscious, subconscious, and unconscious. Almost like real people. The conscious dictates those endless revisions; the subconscious dictates the invention of characters that are pastiches of beloved and/or hated friends, relatives. and acquaintances of the author; and the unconscious does the intricate weaving together of plot and the gathering and distribution of subtext which is the GNP of any real novel.

A writer who lets her conscious dictate subtext and her unconscious the revisions is in serious trouble. Ministers, rabbis, and politicians consciously (and conscientiously — as well as sententiously) dictate subtext and what they write are sermons and position papers.[5] Unpublished writers allow the revisions to be done by their unconscious mind alone, which is to say they don't change a single word in real time. But the professional writer acknowledges the tripartite division and, like Gaul, manages to keep running nonetheless.

As aside: if the profession takes over the writer, a new equation emerges. Deadlines D and payments P are divided by the need to produce stories S and books B. After the equal signs you will find no more elves.

It is easy to see that I believe in the *elf factor,* that sudden appearance on the pages of heretofore unexpected characters or landscapes or pieces of plot machinery. It is what so often distinguishes a piece of writing. I further believe that when something wonderfully anarchic or surprising surfaces, it is the writer's duty to hear the thing out.

Storytelling is always a combination of what we know and what surprises us. But before any reader can be surprised, the author must be surprised, too. Like the sibyls before us, we must be overwhelmed by the vatic voice.

Vatic: the prophetic or oracular or inspired voice. The sibyls used drug-inducing leaves in a smudge pot and the resonant cave walls as conduits for their gnomic utterances. The author, lacking leaves, pot, and cave walls, uses black smudges on a page. I have often said that stories leak out of my fingertips. For me that is a shorthand statement, a metaphor (as in Ciardi's definition of a metaphor as an "exactly felt error") that describes the process of being possessed by the vatic voice.

I am not saying that writers need to put on Indian print dresses, wear dangling earrings, and channel Shirley MacLaine's next book. I am not even saying we need to sit in darkened rooms waiting — like some latter-day William Butler Yeats — for the automatic writing to begin. But we do, indeed, always need to be prepared for serendipity.

Writers, according to Natalie Goldberg in her book *Writing Down the Bones*, "live twice."[6] But that is not entirely true. Writers live twice only when they are prepared to take that second breath, the one that sings out of the chest in the full bardic tones; the one that converses with elves, even when the elves were not in the character list, the plot outline, the 20-page synopsis, or the contract. Even then.

> *And see ye not that bonny road*
> *That winds about the fernie brae?*
> *That is the road to fair Elfland*
> *Where thou and I this night maun gae.*[7]

sings the Elf queen to Thomas of Ercildoune. *Maun* is the operative word here. It means *must*. "Where thou and I must go." He goes with her because he must. Past thorns and briars, past black skies and a sea of blood. Past time itself. Unless and until Thomas of Ercildoune goes with the Elf queen he cannot become the poet, the seer Thomas the Rhymer, he cannot speak truly. In order to become a truth teller, in order to speak *ferly*, you must go with the elf queen, kiss her and go.

Last year when I was living in Edinburgh, I took author Ellen Kushner — who was then working on a novel about

Thomas the Rhymer[8] — on a tour of Erlston and the ruins of
Melrose Abbey. We climbed the Eildon Hills as well. Over-
head was the brilliant blue bowl of sky and beneath our feet the
fern-covered hillside. Writers both, we *were* living twice. As
twentieth-century American women we were clambering up
the gentle slope of the Eildon Hills above a modern farm,
carefully avoiding cowpats. In the Rhymer's Tower Cafe we
had come upon an elderly Scotswoman who had taken us to her
home and recited the 61 verses of "True Thomas" in Broad
Scots while her "auld man" slept by the fire. At the Abbey we
had investigated the remarkably contemporary drainage system and explored the tiny Abbey museum. But we were also at
the same time back in the misty moisty poetic past, 700 years
before, when the Abbey had been filled with the voices of
young men singing psalms, when the hills had been crossed
with roads of thorn and briar, and the Rhymer himself — not
the rhyme — had lived. In that setting neither of us would have
been surprised by elves.

Story is a way of remembering, after all. Once upon a time
is not a specific era; it stands for all time and all times. Just one
letter difference is between *never-never-land* and *ever-ever-land*.
And it is, after all, with exquisite care that someone once called
the land of faerie the place where things never were but always
are.

Grant me, then, that it is important to accept the entrance of
elves. And further understand that if you grant that, you must
be prepared for them as well.

Susan Shwartz, author and academic, has written about
creative research as one way of being prepared. In a letter to me,
she told me about a rather radical Holy Grail book she is writing
in which she suddenly found herself in need of a sister whore for
Mary Magdalene. But she had never read of any specifically.

Something led her to purchase a translation of the Gnostic Gospels and there waiting was something she had no way of knowing existed: a gospel of Mary and a poem "Thunder: Perfect Mind" with a narrative voice that proclaimed itself to be both virgin and whore. "Just," she wrote to me, "what the plot line ordered."

This all sounds suspiciously and wonderfully like Susanne Langer's line about discoveries which she wrote of in *Philosophy in a New Key:*[9] "Most discoveries are suddenly seen things that were always there."

Suddenly seen things. Like Koestler's "shaking together of two previously unconnected matrices,"[10] like the Gestalt therapy's great a-ha, like Watson on the top level of the double-decker bus suddenly envisioning DNA's double helix. Writers need to be prepared for serendipity, must be ready for the entrance of the elves.

This has happened to me enough times so that I look forward to such things. But as they occur differently each time, I am sometimes not as prepared as I might like to be.

For example, in a humorous fantasy novel for children called *Hobo Toad & The Motorcycle Gang*,[11] I wrote about a hitchhiking toad called HT or Hopalong Toad, who gets a ride with a truck driver. Now the driver's truck was filled with — of all things — marbles. It was a throw-away line. I had to fill the truck with something. I had no plans for the truck's contents — at least as far as I knew consciously. But later on, when the motorcycle gang has kidnapped HT and the trucker and several other people along the way, it is that truck full of marbles that actually saves the day. I could have filled the truck with pizzas or chocolate milk or nitroglycerine for that matter. But I stuck a load of marbles, round and ready, in at the loading dock. And when I needed them, the marbles — like the elves — marched onto the scene.

Then there was a fairy tale I wrote called *The Seeing Stick*.[12] It is set in ancient Peking, where a blind princess, unhappy with her lot, is taught to see with her fingers by an old man who comes up from the south. The old man carves his adventures onto a walking stick and teaches the princess, finger on finger, to read this early braille. When I read the story to my writing group — a weekly critique group with which I have been meeting for 19 years — one member said, "I am sorry, did I miss it? Is the old man blind, too?" Stunned, I didn't answer for a second, then blurted out, "Well, of course." Of course he hadn't been the moment before but all the clues had been put in by my unconscious mind. And the book *now* ends:

> As the princess grew, she grew eyes on the tips of her fingers, or at least that is what she told the other blind children whom she taught to see as she saw. And certainly it was as true as saying she had a seeing stick.
>
> But the little blind princess believed that both things were true.
>
> And so did all the blind children in Peking.
> And so did the blind old man.

I also had the experience with a children's novel[13] about the Holocaust, in which a modern-day American girl, Hannah Stern, travels back in time through the door that opens for that estimable time traveler Elijah. When Hannah and her new friends in the shtetl are rounded up by the Nazis and put in a concentration camp, she loses all sense of who she was and now only knows who she *is*, *Chaya Abramowitz*. Well within the nightmare months, she is told a story by the rabbi's daughter. When I got to that part of the novel, I knew I needed a powerful story, a folk tale or midrash tale that would speak to the horror in which they were all bound. I have a number of volumes of Jewish and Israeli folk material. The Yiddish Book Center is in the next town. The problem was to find the right story and yet not spend the next few months researching, because I was afraid of losing the flow of the book. I picked out all the volumes in my library and piled them on my desk. Now this next will seem like mystical claptrap and yet it is exactly what happened. I shuffled through the books and picked out one of them — *Classic Hassidic Tales*. [14] I opened it up randomly and found a story called "Israel and the Enemy" about Rabbi Israel Baal Shem, who takes the heart out of a werewolf and sets it upon the ground. And I knew that I had found the story I needed without opening a single other book. With only slight paraphrasing, I set the story into the mouth of the rabbi's daughter and it summed up in horrifying detail what the people of Chaya's shtetl were going through.

> That night Fayge began to speak, as if the words so long dammed up had risen to flood. She told a story she had heard from her father, about the great Ba'al Shem Tov. It was set in the time when he was a boy named Israel and *his* father warned him: "Know, my son, that the enemy will always be with you. He will be in the shadow of your dreams and in your living flesh, for he is the other part of yourself. There will be times when he will surround you with walls of darkness. But remember always that your soul is secure to you, for your soul is entire, and that he cannot enter your soul, for your soul is part of God." Fayge's voice rose and fell as she told how young Israel led a small band of children against a werewolf whose

heart was Satan's. And in the end, when Israel walked straight into the werewolf's body and held its awful dark heart in his hand, "shivering and jerking like a fish out of water," Fayge said, her own hand moving in the same way, that awful heart was filled with "immeasurable pain. A pain that began before time and would endure forever."

She whispered the story as the night enfolded them. "Then Israel took pity on the heart and gave it freedom. He placed it upon the earth and the earth opened and swallowed the black heart into itself."

A sigh ran around the barrack and Hannah's was the deepest of all. A *werewolf*, she thought. *That's where we are now. In the belly of the werewolf. But where, where is its dark pain-filled heart?* She was still sighing when she slipped into sleep.

A plot device, a character, and a story within a story that serves as metaphor for the entire book — that is what I had become used to.

So why, when the elves marched onto the scene in *White Jenna*, did I balk? For balk I did. I left Jenna and her companions surrounded by a ring of elves for three weeks while I went off and did the usual writer-not-working things. I cleaned the house, I baked cookies, I washed windows, I answered long overdue mail.

I think it has to do with the perception of elves and their place in the world of fantasy literature.

Elfy-welfy is a phrase often heard today in the reviewing of fantasy literature. It summarizes a tendency of rather ardent fans and collectors of badly wrought miniatures to rhapsodize over the Cute. When the line thins down between sentiment and the sentimental, it does not take seven-league boots to cross over.

But if a writer is one who first is an accurate observer and then a careful selector of details, what can we say about the sentimentalist except that he has neither a keen eye nor any understanding of how details work. The sentimentalist softens details or perhaps he first observes them through a fuzzy lens. For if we are to look back upon elves in the lore, we do not find anything cute about them at all.

Dr. H. R. Ellis Davidson in *Scandinavian Mythology*[15] links elves and the dead, suggesting also that their beauty and their dangerous personalities had to do with their being land spirits not always to be counted upon. Something of this latter, she further suspects, came down into the smaller "tricksy flower-loving creatures" of the Elizabethan plays.

Katharine Briggs, the dean of the British folklorists and surely the most knowledgeable folklorist in the realm of the faery folk, reminds us of faery morality, which is not like mortal choosing. Though they will never tell a direct lie, or break a promise, they may "often distort it." And, she further states, "Order more than morality is part of the fairy code. They are great lovers of cleanliness, tidyness and established ways. The second thing they require of human beings is liberality... [they] set high value on courtesy and respect... A flavor of bawdiness hung about them...and a genial rogue is as likely to receive their favours as anyone else." She further points out that elves and other faery folk have no respect for human goods, for "honesty means nothing to [them]. They consider that they have right to whatever they need or fancy, including the human beings themselves."[16]

This is a far cry from the coy pointy-eared creatures in fur loin clothes who have recently infested the shores of fantasy, a vulgarization encouraged by Victorian spiritualists, helped on by Walt Disney, and given a genial pat on the head by Mr. Spock.

Is it any wonder that an Author who discovers elves marching into her hitherto pristine glade chooses to run off to the kitchen and eat chocolate chip cookies until the pesky critters depart for Elfhame?

Three weeks is a long time to consider the inevitable. In the end, of course, I capitulated. Besides, I am nothing if not nosey. I wanted to know what the elves thought they were doing there. The only way to find out was to let them talk. And I could always delete them after. Being an *American* writer, I had to consider them innocent until otherwise proven. I let them walk and talk and lead my Jenna and her party down the primrose paths.

It should be no surprise at this point to any of us that the elves — or at least the forest folk or Green folk or Grenna as it seems they were called — turned out to be important to my book. In fact they turned out to be important to the book that immediately preceded *White Jenna* as well, a book called *Sister Light, Sister Dark*, a book already published.

The Grenna solved three problems raised in the two books: a problem of time, a problem of sociological structures, and a problem that had to do with pre-history metaphysics, if you will. Only one of these was a problem I knew I had.

The problem of time was clear. I had as my hero a fourteen-year-old girl. I was a third of the way through the second book and she needed to be much older. But I hadn't the time — literally — in the novel to let all that time pass. And it wasn't the kind of book where you could keep them on their horses for another five years. That would be a "Long Riding" indeed.

The first chapter in Katharine Briggs's book *The Vanishing People: Fairy Lore & Legends*, a book I consulted regularly when working on notes for my mammoth collection of *Folk Tales From Around the World* for Pantheon, is called "The Supernatural Passage of Time in Fairyland." It begins:

> All through the world, wherever the idea of Fairyland or of a supernatural country was evolved, it was accompanied by a strong feeling of the relativity of time. This may well have been founded on the experiences of a dream or a state of trance. It is common in a dream to pass through long and varied experiences in the mortal time occupied between, let us say, beginning to fall out of bed and landing with a bump on the floor. In a state of trance, on the other hand, the mental processes can be so retarded that one train of thought is slowly pursued for several hours. Both these psychological experiences are reproduced in legends of visits to fairyland or to the Other World.[17]

What better use of my new elven characters than to have them take Jenna and company to their own world — below the hill or into the glade or through the tunnel, all viable folkloric concepts — where time will move differently: When my travelers emerge, it is five years (but only 14 pages) later.

The problem of sociologic structure was less clear, but somehow these Green Folk did not live in a hierarchical society. Unlike the usual folkloric elves whose highly structured society always consists of a queen or king at the top, a royal or seely (seelie) court, and fairy underlings, with human or changeling others at the bottom, my elves announced: "We have neither king nor captain. We have only the circle." And later add, "Is the circle not the perfect form...? ...In it no one is higher. No one is lower. No one is first. No one is last."[18]

It certainly sets up a different form in opposition to the hierarchies within the books' other societal structures, where a king reigns in the land, a captain rules the armies, a priestess or Mother Alta rules the Hames, and Jenna, unwillingly, commands.

The third problem the elves dealt with was to explain in an allegorical way, in the trance state of time manipulation, who the great goddess of the Dales was and how she came to know the magic she knows and why she passed it on to the women of the Dales.

The one thing they do not explain is how and why there are elves. But that is perhaps something to be left for another adventure, another trance, another author. As the spokesman for the elves for that time says: "This one speaks today. Tomorrow another. The circle moves on."[19]

When I listened to my elves, I discovered that they had indeed links with the elven folk of fairy lore. They do have some connection with the dead, for Jenna cannot come back to the land-outside-of-time until she is close to death herself. And the Grenna, while never telling a direct lie, do avoid telling the complete truth. Their circle, being the perfect form, is as neat and tidy as anything elves in the old woods might imagine. Yet they are not simple clones of the old elves. They are couriers, they are transporters, they are device rather than devisers. And as swiftly as they moved onto the pages, they moved off again.

I don't want you to think that what I am talking about has anything to do with New Age shamanism or Madame Blavatsky trance writing. Rather I am trying to draw a distinction between conscious creation and what I term the *elf factor*, that is, the Author's receptivity to surprise.

William Morris wrote: "The master of any trade can keep his eye on the work, what he wants to do, and leave his hand free to get it out. He has it in his mind's eye clearly enough. But when it is finished, his hands put a lot of things into it that his mind never thought of: that is exactly where inspiration comes in, if you want to call it so."[20]

In fact I call it so — at 9 o'clock every morning. And my gates remain open to any passing elves.

1 Yolen, Jane, *White Jenna*, Tor Books, 1989, pp. 43–82.
2 I have tried in vain to track down a citation for this wonderful bit of Faulknerian wisdom, something I have known for years.
3 Yolen, Jane, *White Jenna*, Tor Books, 1989, p. 58.
4 For the complete text of this song, ask Steve Brust, who sings it whenever asked (and sometimes when asked not to) with great glee.
5 Having been a speech writer for a political campaign, I am well aware of the difference between novels and position papers, though fiction is a heavy component of both!
6 Goldberg, Natalie, *Writing Down the Bones*, Shambhala, 1986, p. 4.
7 "Thomas the Rhymer," Child Ballad #37, *The English and Scottish Popular Ballads*, Dover, Vol. 1, 1882, 1965, pp. 317–329.
8 Kushner, Ellen, *Thomas the Rhymer*, Morrow, 1990.
9 Langer, Susanne, *Philosophy in a New Key*, Harvard

University Press, 1951.

10 Koestler, Arthur, *The Act of Creation*, Macmillan, 1964.

11 Yolen, Jane, *Hobo Toad & the Motorcycle Gang*, World, 1970.

12 Yolen, Jane, *The Seeing Stick*, T.Y. Crowell, 1976.

13 Yolen, Jane, *The Devil's Arithmetic*, Viking, 1988.

14 Levin, Meyer, reteller, *Classic Hassidic Tales*, Dorset Press, 1931, 1959, 1985, pp. 10–16.

15 Davidson, Dr. H.R. Ellis, *Scandinavian Mythology*, London, 1967.

16 Briggs, Katharine, *The Fairies in English Tradition and Literature*, University of Chicago Press, 1967, pp. 108–114.

17 Briggs, Katharine, *The Vanishing People*, Pantheon Books, 1978, p. 11.

18 Yolen, Jane, *White Jenna*, Tor Books, 1989, pp. 59-61.

19 Ibid, p. 61.

20 Sparling, H. Halliday, *The Kelmscott Press & William Morris, Master Craftsman*.

My daughter Heidi knows this poem is about her. You should see some of the men she's dated over the years. But isn't there a button that says YOU HAVE TO KISS A LOT OF FROGS BEFORE YOU FIND A PRINCE? Or maybe that's toads.

Frog Prince

It is so hard these days
to find a proper prince.
The world is dappled
with pretenders,
as spotty with them
as an adolescent's skin.
I have three daughters;
I have three wedding portions
waiting, waiting
for the marriage offer.
A kingdom
is but a small return
for fifteen years
of tending
these hothouse plants.
Can one read the heart?
Can one judge the mind?
Can one guess the future
from a handshake by a well,
from a dinner conversation,
from a single night in bed?
Yet my first wants to marry
a drummer in a rock band,
my second a man who works with cars.
What next, I ask you?
A grocer's lad?
        A stable boy?
     An enchanted frog?

MERLE
INSINGA '91

When this story was originally published, someone at the publishing company changed it to "Memoirs of a Bottle Djinni," spoiling the joke. A middle-aged love story, it is dedicated to my husband. Susan Shwartz wanted something for her Arabesques *anthology and this was about as baroque as I could manage.*

Memoirs of a Bottle Djinn

The sea was as dark as old blood, not the wine-color poets sing of. In the early evening it seemed to stain the sand. As usual this time of the year the air was heavy, ill-omened.

I walked out onto the beach below my master's house whenever I could slip away unnoticed, though it was a dangerous practice. Still, it was one necessary to my well-being. I had been a sailor for many more years than I had been a slave and the smell of the salt air was not a luxury for me but a necessity.

If a seabird had washed up dead at my feet, its belly would have contained black worms and other evil auguries, so dark and lowering was the sky. So I wondered little at the bottle that the sea had deposited before me, certain it contained noxious fumes at best, the legacy of its long cradling in such a salty womb.

In my country poets sing the praises of wine and gift its color to the water along the shores of Hellas and I can think of no finer hymn. But in this land they believe their prophet forbade them strong drink. They are a sober race who reward themselves in heaven even as they deny themselves on earth. It is a system of which I do not approve, but then I am a Greek by birth and a heathen by inclination despite my master's long importuning. It is only by chance that I have not yet lost an eye, an ear, or a hand to my master's unforgiving code. He finds me amusing but it has been seven years since I have had a drink.

I stared at the bottle. If I had any luck at all, the bottle had fallen from a foreign ship and its contents would still be potable. But then, if I had any luck at all, I would not be a slave in Araby, a Greek sailor washed up on these shores the same as the bottle at my feet. My father, who was a cynic like his father before him, left me with a cynic's name — Antithias — a wry heart, and an acid tongue, none proper legacies for a slave. But as blind Homer wrote, "Few sons are like their father; many are worse." I guessed that the wine, if drinkable, would come from an inferior year. And with that thought, I bent to pick it up.

The glass was a cloudy green, like the sea after a violent storm. Like the storm that had wrecked my ship and cast me onto a slaver's shore. There were darker flecks along the bottom, a sediment that surely foretold an undrinkable wine. I let the bottle warm between my palms.

Since the glass was too dark to let me see more, I waited past my first desire and was well into my second, letting it rise up in me like the heat of passion. The body has its own memories, though I must be frank: passion, like wine, was simply a fragrance remembered. Slaves are not lent the services of houris, nor was one my age and race useful for breeding. It had only been by feigning impotence that I had kept that part of my anatomy intact — another of my master's unforgiving laws. Even in the dark of night, alone on my own pallet, I forewent the pleasures of the hand, for there were spies everywhere in his house and the eunuchs were a notably gossipy lot. Little but a slave's tongue lauding morality stood between gossip and scandal, stood between me and the knife. Besides, the women of Araby tempted me little. They were like the bottle in my hand — beautiful and empty. A wind blowing across the mouth of each could make them sing, but the tunes were worth little. I liked my women like my wine — full-bodied and tanged with history, bringing a man into poetry. So I had put my passion into work these past seven years, slave's work though it was. Blind Homer had it right, as usual: "Labor conquers all things." Even old lusts for women and wine.

Philosophy did not conquer movement, however, and my hand found the cork of the bottle before I could stay it. With one swift movement I had plucked the stopper out. A thin strand of smoke rose into the air. A very bad year indeed, I thought, as the cork crumbled into my hand.

Up and up and up the smoky rope ascended and I, bottle in hand, could not move, such was my disappointment. Even my father's cynicism and his father's before him had not prepared me for such a sudden loss of all hope. My mind, a moment before full of anticipation and philosophy, was now in blackest despair. I found myself without will, reliving in my mind the moment of my capture and the first bleak days of my enslavement.

That is why it was several minutes before I realized that the smoke had begun to assume a recognizable shape above the bottle's gaping mouth: long, sensuous legs glimpsed through diaphanous trousers; a waist my hands could easily span; breasts beneath a short embroidered cotton vest as round as ripe pomegranates; and a face...the face was smoke and air. I remembered suddenly a girl in the port of Alexandria who sold fruit from a basket and gave me a smile. She was the last girl who had smiled upon me when I was a free man and I, not knowing the future, had ignored her, so intent was I on my work. My eyes clouded over at the memory, and when they were clear again, I saw that same smile imprinted upon the face of the djinn.

"I am what you would have me be, master," her low voice called down to me.

I reached up a hand to help her step to earth, but my hand went through hers, mortal flesh through smoky air. It was then, I think, that I really believed she was what I guessed her to be.

She smiled. "What is your wish, master?"

I took the time to smile back. "How many wishes do I get?"

She shook her head but still she smiled, that Alexandrian smile, all lips without a hint of teeth. But there was a dimple in her left cheek. "One, my master, for you drew the cork but once."

"And if I draw it again?"

"The cork is gone." This time her teeth showed, as did a second dimple, on the right.

I sighed and looked at the crumbled mess in my hand, then sprinkled the cork like seed upon the sand. "Just one."

"Does a slave need more?" she asked in that same low voice.

"You mean that I should ask for my freedom?" I laughed and sat down on the strand. The little waves that outrun the big ones tickled my feet, for I had come out barefoot. I looked across the water. "Free to be a sailor again at my age? Free to let the sun peel the skin from my back, free to heave my guts over the stern in a blinding rain, free to wreck once more upon a slaver's shore?"

She drifted down beside me and though her smoky hand could not hold mine, I felt a breeze across my palm that could have been her touch. I could see through her to the cockleshells and white stones pocking the sand.

"Free to make love to Alexandrian women," she said. "Free to drink strong wine."

"Free to have regrets in the morning either way," I replied. Then I laughed.

She laughed back. "What about the freedom to indulge in a dinner of roast partridge in lemons and eggplant? What about hard-boiled eggs sprinkled with vermilion? What about cinnamon tripes?" It was the meal my master had just had.

"Rich foods, like rich women, give me heartburn," I said.

"The freedom to fill your pockets with coins?"

Looking away from her, over the clotted sea, I whispered to myself, " 'Accursed thirst for gold! What dost thou not compel mortals to do,' " a line from the *Aeneid.*

"Virgil was a wise man," she said quietly. "For a Roman!" Then she laughed.

I turned to look at her closely for the first time. A woman who knows Virgil, be she djinn or mortal, was a woman to behold. Though her body was still composed of that shifting, smoky air, the features on her face now held steady. She no longer looked like the Alexandrian girl, but had a far more sophisticated beauty. Lined with kohl, her eyes were grey as smoke and her hair the same color. There were shadows along her cheeks that emphasized the bone and faint smile lines crinkling the skin at each corner of her generous mouth. She was not as young as she had first appeared, but then I am not so young myself.

"Ah, Antithias," she said, smiling at me, "even djinn age, though being corked up in a bottle slows the process immensely."

I spoke Homer's words to her then: " 'In youth and beauty, wisdom is but rare.' " I added in my own cynic's way, "If ever."

"You think me wise, then?" she asked, then laughed — and her laughter was like the tinkling of camel bells. "But a gaudy parrot is surely as wise, reciting another's words as his own."

"I know no parrots who hold Virgil and Homer in their mouths," I said, gazing at her not with longing but with a kind of wonder. "No djinn either."

"You know many?"

"Parrots, yes; djinn, no. You are my first."

"Then you are lucky, indeed, Greek, that you called up one of the worshippers of Allah and not one of the followers of Iblis."

I nodded. "Lucky indeed."

"So to your wish, master," she said.

"You call me master, I who am a slave," I said. "Do *you* not want the freedom you keep offering me? Freedom from the confining green bottle, freedom from granting wishes to any *master* who draws the cork?"

She brushed her silvery hair back from her forehead with a delicate hand. "You do not understand the nature of the djinn," she said. "You do not understand the nature of the bottle."

"I understand rank," I said. "On the sea I was between the captain and the rowers. In that house" — and I gestured with my head to the palace behind me — "I am below my master and above the kitchen staff. Where are you?"

Her brow furrowed as she thought. "If I work my wonders for centuries, I might at last attain a higher position within the djinn," she said.

It was my turn to smile. "Rank is a game," I said. "It may be conferred by birth, by accident, or by design. But rank does not honor the man. The man honors the rank."

"You are a philosopher," she said, her eyes lightening.

"I am a Greek," I answered. "It is the same thing."

She laughed again, holding her palm over her mouth coquettishly. I could no longer see straight through her, though an occasional piece of driftweed appeared like a delicate tattoo on her skin.

"Perhaps we both need a wish," I said, shifting my weight. One of my feet touched hers and I could feel a slight jolt, as though lightning had run between us. Such things happen occasionally on the open sea.

"Alas, I cannot wish myself," she said in a whisper. "I can only grant wishes."

I looked at her lovely face washed with its sudden sadness and whispered back, "Then I give my wish to you."

She looked directly into my eyes and I could see her eyes

turn golden in the dusky light. I could at the same time somehow see beyond them, not into the sand or water, but to a different place, a place of whirlwinds and smokeless fire.

"Then, Antithias, you will have wasted a wish," she said. Shifting her gaze slightly, she looked behind me, her eyes opening wide in warning. As she spoke, her body seemed to melt into the air and suddenly there was a great white bird before me, beating its feathered pinions against my body before taking off towards the sky.

"Where are you going?" I cried.

"To the Valley of Abqar," the bird called. "To the home of my people. I will wait there for your wish, Greek. But hurry. I see both your past and your future closing in behind you."

I turned and, pouring down the stone steps of my master's house, were a half dozen guards and one shrilling eunuch pointing his flabby hand in my direction. They came towards me screaming, though what they were saying I was never to know, for their scimitars were raised and my Arabic deserts me in moments of sheer terror.

I think I screamed; I am not sure. But I spun around again towards the sea and saw the bird winging away in a halo of light.

"Take me with you," I cried. "I desire no freedom but by your side."

The bird shuddered as it flew, then banked sharply, and headed back towards me, calling, "Is that your wish, master?"

A scimitar descended.

"That is my wish," I cried, as the blade bit into my throat.

We have lived now for centuries within the green bottle and Zarifa was right, I had not understood its nature. Inside is an entire world, infinite and ever-changing. The smell of the salt air blows through that world and we dwell in a house that sometimes overlooks the ocean and sometimes overlooks the desert sands.

Zarifa, my love, is as mutable, neither young nor old, neither soft nor hard. She knows the songs of blind Homer and the poet Virgil as well as the poems of the warlords of Ayyam Al-'Arab. She can sing in languages that are long dead.

And she loves me beyond my wishing, or so she says, and I must believe it for she would not lie to me. She loves me though I have no great beauty, my body bearing a sailor's scars and a slave's scars and this curious blood necklace where the scimitar left its mark. She loves me, she says, for my cynic's wit and my noble heart, that I would have given my wish to her.

So we live together in our ever-changing world. I read now in six tongues beside Greek and Arabic, and have learned to paint and sew. My paintings are in the Persian style, but I embroider like a Norman queen. We learn from the centuries, you see, and we taste the world anew each time the cork is drawn.

So there, my master, I have fulfilled your curious wish, speaking my story to you alone. It seems a queer waste of your one piece of luck, but then most men waste their wishes. And if you are a poet and a storyteller, as you say, of the lineage of blind Homer and the rest, but one who has been blocked from telling more tales, then perhaps my history can speed you on your way again. I shall pick up one of your old books, my master, now that we have a day and a night in this new world. Do you have a favorite I should try — or should I just go to a bookseller and trust my luck? In the last few centuries it has been remarkably good, you see.

This story was the second one I wrote for Guinevere's Booke. *Alas — the original publisher was not interested. Any small press people out there game?*

The Quiet Monk

Glastonbury Abbey, in the year of Our Lord 1191

He was a tall man, and his shoulders looked broad even under the shapeless disguise of the brown sacking. The hood hid the color of his hair and, when he pushed the hood back, the tonsure was so close cropped, he might have been a blonde or a redhead or gray. It was his eyes that held one's interest most. They were the kind of blue that I had only seen on midsummer skies, with the whites the color of bleached muslin. He was a handsome man, with a strong, thin nose and a mouth that would make all the women in the parish sure to shake their heads with the waste of it. They were a lusty lot, the parish dames, so I had been warned.

I was to be his guide as I was the spryest of the brothers, even with my twisted leg, for I was that much younger than the rest, being newly come to my vocation, one of the few infant oblates who actually joined that convocation of saints. Most left to go into trade, though a few, it must be admitted, joined the army, safe in their hearts for a peaceful death.

Father Joseph said I was not to call the small community "saints," for sainthood must be earned not conferred, but my birth father told me, before he gave me to the abbey, that by living in such close quarters with saintly men I could become one. And that he, by gifting me, would win a place on high. I am not sure if all this was truly accomplished, for my father died of a disease his third wife brought to their marriage bed, a strange wedding portion indeed. And mostly my time in the abbey was taken up not in prayer side by side with saints but on my knees cleaning the abbot's room, the long dark halls, and the *dortoir*. Still, it was better than being back at home in Meade's Hall, where I was the butt of every joke, no matter I was the son of the lord. His eighth son, born twisted ankle to thigh, the murderer of his own mother at the hard birthing. At least in Glastonbury Abbey I was needed, if not exactly loved.

So when the tall wanderer knocked on the door late that Sunday night, and I was the watcher at the gate, Brother Sanctus being abed with a shaking fever, I got to see the quiet monk first.

It is wrong, I know, to love another man in that way. It is wrong to worship a fellow human even above God. It is the one great warning dunned into infant oblates from the start. For a boy's heart is a natural altar and many strange deities ask for sacrifice there. But I loved him when first I saw him for the hope I saw imprinted on his face and the mask of sorrow over it.

He did not ask to come in; he demanded it. But he never raised his voice nor spoke other than quietly. That is why we dubbed him the Quiet Monk and rarely used his name. Yet he owned a voice with more authority than even Abbot Giraldus could command, for *he* is a shouter. Until I met the Quiet Monk, I had quaked at the abbot's bluster. Now I know it for what it truly is: fear masquerading as power.

"I seek a quiet corner of your abbey and a word with your abbot after his morning prayers and ablutions," the Quiet Monk said.

I opened the gate, conscious of the squawking lock and the cries of the wood as it moved. Unlike many abbeys, we had no rooms ready for visitors. Indeed we never entertained guests anymore. We could scarce feed ourselves these days. But I did not tell *him* that. I led him to my own room, identical to all the others save the abbot's, which was even meaner, as Abbot Giraldus reminded us daily. The Quiet Monk did not seem to notice, but nodded silently and eased himself onto my thin pallet, falling asleep at once. Only soldiers and monks have such a facility. My father, who once led a cavalry, had it. And I, since coming to the abbey, had it, too. I covered him gently with my one thin blanket and crept from the room.

In the morning, the Quiet Monk talked for a long time with Abbot Giraldus and then with Fathers Joseph and Paul. He joined us in our prayers, and when we sang, his voice leaped over the rest, even over the sopranos of the infant oblates and the lovely tenor of Brother John. He stayed far longer on his knees than any, at the last prostrating himself on the cold stone floor for over an hour. That caused the abbot much distress, which manifested itself in a tantrum aimed at my skills at cleaning. I had to rewash the floor in the abbot's room where the stones were already smooth from his years of penances.

Brother Denneys — for so was the Quiet Monk's name, called he said after the least of boys who shook him out of a dream of apathy — was given leave to stay until a certain task was accomplished. But before the task could be done, permission would have to be gotten from the pope.

What that task was to be, neither the abbot nor Fathers Joseph or Paul would tell. And if I wanted to know, the only one I might turn to was Brother Denneys himself. Or I could wait until word came from the Holy Father, which word — as we all knew full well — might take days, weeks, even months over the slow roads between Glastonbury and Rome. If word came at all.

Meanwhile, Brother Denneys was a strong back and a stronger hand. And wonder of wonders (a miracle, said Father Joseph, who did not parcel out miracles with any regularity), he also had a deep pocket of gold which he shared with Brother

Aermand, who cooked our meagre meals. As long as Brother
Denneys remained at the abbey, we all knew we would eat
rather better than we had in many a year. Perhaps that is why
it took so long for word to come from the Pope. So it was our
small convocation of saints became miners, digging gold out of
a particular seam. Not all miracles, Father Joseph had once said,
proceed from a loving heart. Some, he had mused, come from
too little food or too much wine or not enough sleep. And, I
added to myself, from too great a longing for gold.

Ours was not a monastery where silence was the rule. We had
so little else, talk was our one great privilege, except of course
on holy days, which there were rather too many of. As was our
custom, we foregathered at meals to share the day's small
events: the plants beginning to send through their green
hosannahs, the epiphanies of birds' nest, and the prayerful bits
of gossip any small community collects. It was rare we talked of
our pasts. The past is what had driven most of us to Glastonbury.
Even Saint Patrick, that most revered of holy men, it was said,
came to Glastonbury posting ahead of his long past. Our little
wattled church had heard the confessions of good men and bad,
saints of passing fairness and sinners of surprising depravity,
before it had been destroyed seven years earlier by fire. But the
stories that Brother Denneys told us that strange spring were
surely the most surprising confessions of all, and I read in the
expressions of the abbot and Fathers Joseph and Paul a sudden
overwhelming greed that surpassed all understanding.

What Brother Denneys rehearsed for us were the matters
that had set him wandering: a king's wife betrayed, a friendship
destroyed, a repentance sought, and over the many years a
driving need to discover the queen's grave, that he might plead
for forgiveness at her crypt. But all this was not new to the
father confessors who had listened to lords and ploughmen

alike. It was the length of time he had been wandering that surprised us.

Of course we applauded his despair and sanctified his search with a series of oratories sung by our choir. Before the church had burned down, we at Glastonbury had been noted for our voices, one of the three famed perpetual choirs, the others being at Caer Garadawg and at Bangor. I sang the low ground bass, which surprised everyone who saw me, for I am thin and small with a chest many a martyr might envy. But we were rather fewer voices than we might have been seven years previously, the money for the church repair having gone instead to fund the Crusades. Fewer voices — and quite a few skeptics, though the abbot, and Fathers Paul and Joseph, all of whom were in charge of our worldly affairs, were quick to quiet the doubters because of that inexhaustible pocket of gold.

How long had he wandered? Well, he certainly did not look his age. Surely six centuries should have carved deeper runes on his brow and shown the long bones. But in the end, there was not a monk at Glastonbury, including even Brother Thomas, named after that doubting forebear, who remained unconvinced.

Brother Denneys revealed to us that he had once been a knight, the fairest of that fair company of Christendom who had accompanied the mighty King Arthur in his search for the grail.

"I who was Lancelot du Lac," he said, his voice filled with that quiet authority, "am now but a wandering mendicant. I seek the grave of that sweetest lady whom I taught to sin, skin upon skin, tongue into mouth like fork into meat."

If we shivered deliciously at the moment of the telling, who can blame us, especially those infant oblates just entering their manhood. Even Abbot Giraldus forgot to cross himself, so moved was he by the confession.

But all unaware of the stir he was causing, Brother Denneys

continued.

"She loved the king, you know, but not the throne. She loved the man of him, but not the monarch. He did not know how to love a woman. He husbanded a kingdom, you see. It was enough for him. He should have been a saint."

He was silent then, as if in contemplation. We were all silent, as if he had set us a parable that we would take long years unraveling, as scholars do a tale.

A sigh from his mouth, like the wind over an old unused well, recalled us. He did not smile. It was as if there were no smiles left in him, but he nodded and continued.

"What does a kingdom need but to continue? What does a queen need but to bear an heir?" He paused, not to hear the questions answered but to draw deep breath. He went on. "I swear that was all that drove her into my arms, not any great adulterous love for me. Oh, for a century or two I still fancied ours was the world's great love, a love borne on the wings of magic first and then the necromancy of passion alone. I cursed and blamed that witch Morgaine even as I thanked her. I cursed and blamed the stars. But in the end I knew myself a fool, for no man is more foolish than when he is misled by his own base maunderings." He gestured downward with his hand, dismissing the lower half of his body, bit his lip as if in memory, then spoke again.

"When she took herself to Amesbury Convent, I knew the truth but would not admit it. Lacking the hope of a virgin birth, she had chosen me — not God — to fill her womb. In that I failed her even as God had. She could not hold my seed; I could not plant a healthy crop. There was one child that came too soon, a tailed infant with bulging eyes, more *mer* than human. After that there were no more." He shivered.

I shivered.

We all shivered, thinking on that monstrous child.

"When she knew herself a sinner, who had sinned without result, she committed herself to sanctity alone, like the man she worshipped, the husband she adored. I was forgot."

One of the infant oblates chose that moment to sigh out loud, and the abbot threw him a dark look, but Brother Denneys never heard.

"Could I do any less than she?" His voice was so quiet then, we all strained forward in the pews to listen. "Could I strive to forget my sinning self? I had to match her passion for passion, and so I gave my sin to God." He stood and with one swift, practiced movement pulled off his robe and threw himself naked onto the stone floor.

I do not know what others saw, but I was so placed that I could not help but notice. From the back, where he lay full length upon the floor, he was a well-muscled man. But from the front he was as smoothly wrought as a girl. In some frenzy of misplaced penitence in the years past, he had cut his manhood from him, dedicating it — God alone knew where — on an altar of despair.

I covered my face with my hands and wept; wept for his pain and for his hopelessness and wept that I, crooked as I was, could not follow him on his long, lonely road.

We waited for months for word to come from Rome, but either the Holy Father was too busy with the three quarrelsome kings and their Crusades, or the roads between Glastonbury and Rome were closed, as usual, by brigands. At any rate, no message came, and still the Quiet Monk worked at the abbey, paying for the privilege out of his inexhaustible pocket. I spent as much time as I could working by his side, which meant I often did double and triple duty. But just to hear his soft voice rehearsing the tales of his past was enough for me. Dare I say it? I preferred his stories to the ones in the Gospels. They had all the beauty, the magic, the mystery, and one thing more. They had a human passion, a life such as I could never attain.

One night, long after the winter months were safely past and the sun had warmed the abbey gardens enough for our spades to snug down easily between the rows of last year's plantings, Brother Denneys came into my cell. Matins was past for the night and such visits were strictly forbidden.

"My child," he said quietly, "I would talk with you."

"Me?" My voice cracked as it had not this whole year past. "Why me?" I could feel my heart beating out its own canonical hours, but I was not so far from my days as an infant oblate that I could not at the same time keep one ear tuned for footsteps in the hall.

"You, Martin," he said, "because you listen to my stories and follow my every move with the eyes of a hound to his master or a squire his knight."

I looked down at the stone floor unable to protest, for he was right. It was just that I had not known he had noticed my faithfulness.

"Will you do something for me if I ask it?"

"Even if it were to go against God and his saints," I whispered. "Even then."

"Even if it were to go against Abbot Giraldus and his rule?"

"Especially then," I said under my breath, but he heard.

Then he told me what had brought him specifically to Glastonbury, the secret which he had shared with the abbot and Fathers Paul and Joseph, the reason he waited for word from Rome that never came.

"There was a bard, a Welshman, with a voice like a demented dove, who sang of this abbey and its graves. But there are many abbeys and many acres of stones throughout this land. I have seen them all. Or so I thought. But in his rhymes — and in his cups — he spoke of Glastonbury's two pyramids with the

grave between. His song had a ring of Merlin's truth in it, which
that mage had spoke long before the end of our tale: *'a little
green, a private peace, between the standing stones.'* "

I must have shaken my head, for he began to recite a poem
with the easy familiarity of the mouth which sometimes remembers what the mind has forgot.

> *A time will come when what is three makes one:*
> *A little green, a private peace, between the standing stones.*
> *A gift of gold shall betray the place at a touch.*
> *Absolution rests upon its mortal couch.*

He spoke with absolute conviction, but the whole spell made
less sense to me than the part. I did not answer him.

He sighed. "You do not understand. The grave between
those stone pyramids is the one I seek. I am sure of it now. But
your abbot is adamant. I cannot have permission to unearth the
tomb without a nod from Rome. Yet I must open it, Martin, I
must. She is buried within and I must throw myself at her dear
dead feet and be absolved." He had me by the shoulders.

"Pyramids?" I was not puzzled by his passion or by his utter
conviction that he had to untomb his queen. But as far as I
knew there were no pyramids in the abbey's yard.

"There are two tapered plinths," Brother Denneys said.
"With carvings on them. A whole roster of saints." He shook
my shoulders as if to make me understand.

Then I knew what he meant. Or at least I knew the plinths
to which he referred. They looked little like pyramids. They
were large standing tablets on which the names of the abbots
of the past and other godly men of this place ran down the side
like rainfall. It took a great imagining — or a greater need —
to read a pair of pyramids there. And something more. I *had* to
name it.

"There is no grave there, Brother Denneys. Just a sward, green in the spring and summer, no greener place in all the boneyard. We picnic there once a year to remember God's gifts."

"That is what I hoped. That is how Merlin spoke the spell. A *little green*. A *private peace*. My lady's place would be that green."

"But there is nothing there!" On this one point I would be adamant.

"You do not know that, my son. And my hopes are greater than your knowledge." There was a strange cast to his eyes that I could just see, for a sliver of moonlight was lighting my cell. "Will you go with me when the moon is full, just two days hence? I cannot dig it alone. Someone must needs stand guardian."

"Against whom?"

"Against the mist maidens, against the spirits of the dead."

"I can only stand against the abbot and those who watch at night." I did not add that I could also take the blame. He was a man who brought out the martyr in me. Perhaps that was what had happened to his queen.

"Will you?"

I looked down the bed at my feet, outlined under the thin blanket in the same moonlight. My right foot was twisted so severely that, even disguised with the blanket, it was grotesque. I looked up at him, perched on my bedside. He was almost smiling at me.

"I will," I said. "God help me, I will."

He embraced me once, rose, and left the room.

How slowly, how quickly those two days flew by. I made myself stay away from his side as if by doing so I could avert all suspicion from our coming deed. I polished the stone floors along the hall until one of the infant oblates, young Christopher of Chedworth, slipped and fell badly enough to have to remain the day under the infirmarer's care. The abbot removed me from my duties and set me to hoeing the herb beds and washing the pots as penance.

And the Quiet Monk did not speak to me again, nor even nod as he passed, having accomplished my complicity. Should we have known that all we did *not* do signaled even more clearly our intent? Should Brother Denneys, who had been a man of battle, have plotted better strategies? I realize now that as a knight he had been a solitary fighter. As a lover, he had been caught out at his amours. Yet even then, even when I most certainly was denying Him, God was looking over us and smoothing the stones in our paths.

Matins was done and I had paid scant attention to the psalms and even less to the antiphons. Instead I watched the moon as it shone through the chapel window, illuminating the glass picture of Lazarus rising from the dead. Twice Brother Thomas had elbowed me into the proper responses and three times Father Joseph had glared down at me from above.

But Brother Denneys never once gave me the sign I awaited, though the moon made a full halo over the lazar's head.

Dejected, I returned to my cell and flung myself onto my knees, a position that was doubly painful to me because of my bad leg, and prayed to the God I had neglected to deliver me from false hopes and wicked promises.

And then I heard the slap of sandals coming down the hall. I did not move from my knees, though the pains shot up my right leg and into my groin. I waited, taking back all the prayers I had sent heavenward just moments before, and was rewarded for my faithlessness by the sight of the Quiet Monk striding into my cell.

He did not have to speak. I pulled myself up without his help, smoothed down the skirts of my cassock so as to hide my crooked leg, and followed him wordlessly down the hall.

It was silent in the dark *dortoir,* except for the noise of Brother Thomas's strong snores and a small pop-pop-popping sound that punctuated the sleep of the infant oblates. I knew that later that night, the novice master would check on the sleeping boys, but he was not astir now. Only the gatekeeper was alert, snug at the front gate and waiting for a knock from Rome that might never come. But we were going out the back door and into the graveyard. No one would hear us there.

Brother Denneys had a great shovel ready by the door. Clearly, he had been busy while I was on my knees. I owed him silence and duty. And my love.

We walked side by side through the cemetery, threading our way past many headstones. He slowed his natural pace to my limping one, though I know he yearned to move ahead rapidly. I thanked him silently and worked hard to keep up.

There were no mist maidens, no white-robed ghosts moaning aloud beneath the moon, nor had I expected any. I knew more than most how the mind conjures up monsters. So often jokes had been played upon me as a child, and a night in the boneyard was a favorite in my part of the land, Many a chilly moon I had been left in our castle graveyard, tied up in an open pit or laid flat on a new slab. My father used to laugh at the pranks. He may even have paid the pranksters. After all, he was a great believer in the toughened spirit. But I like to think he was secretly proud that I never complained. I had often been cold and the ache settled permanently in my twisted bones, but I was never abused by ghosts and so did not credit them.

All these memories and more marched across my mind as I followed Brother Denneys to the pyramids that bordered his hopes.

There were no ghosts, but there *were* shadows, and more than once we both leaped away from them, until we came at last to the green, peaceful place where the Quiet Monk believed his lost love lay buried.

"I will dig," he said, "and you will stand there as guard."

He pointed to a spot where I could see the dark outlines of both church and housing, and in that way know quickly if anyone was coming toward us this night. So while he dug, in his quiet, competent manner, I climbed up upon a cold stone dedicated to a certain Brother Silas, and kept the watch.

The only accompaniment to the sound of his spade thudding into the sod was the long, low whinny of a night owl on the hunt and the scream of some small animal that signaled the successful end. After that, there was only the soft *thwack-thwack* of the spade biting deeper and deeper into the dirt of that unproved grave.

He must have dug for hours; I had only the moon to mark the passage of time. But he was well down into the hole with but the crown of his head showing when he cried out.

I ran over to the edge of the pit and stared down.

"What is it?" I asked, staring between the black shadows.

"Some kind of wood," he said.

"A coffin?"

"More like the barrel of a tree," he said. He bent over. "Definitely a tree. Oak, I think."

"Then your bard was wrong," I said. "But then, he was a Welshman."

"It is a Druid burial," he said. "That is what the oak means. Merlin would have fixed it up."

"I thought Merlin died first. Or disappeared. You told me that. In one of your stories."

He shook his head. "It is a Druid trick, no doubt of it. You will see." He started digging again, this time at a much faster pace, the dirt sailing backwards and out of the pit, covering my sandals before I moved. A fleck of it hit my eye and made me cry. I was a long while digging it out, a long while weeping.

"That's it, then," came his voice. "And there's more besides."

I looked over into the pit once again. "More?"

"Some sort of stone, with a cross on the bottom side."

"Because she was Christian?" I asked.

He nodded. "The Druids had to give her that. They gave her little else."

The moon was mostly gone, but a thin line of light stretched tight across the horizon. I could hear the first bells from the abbey, which meant Brother Angelus was up and ringing them. If we were not at prayers, they would look for us. If we were not in our cells alone, I knew they would come out here. Abbot Giraldus might have been a blusterer but he was not a stupid man.

"Hurry," I said.

He turned his face up to me and smiled. "All these years waiting," he said. "All these years hoping. All these years of false graves." Then he turned back and, using the shovel as a pry, levered open the oak cask.

Inside were the remains of two people, not one, with the bones intertwined, as if in death they embraced with more passion than in life. One was clearly a man's skeleton, with the long bones of the legs fully half again the length of the other's. There was a helm such as a fighting man might wear lying crookedly near the skull. The other skeleton was marked with fine gold braids of hair, that caught the earliest bit of daylight.

"Guenivere," the Quiet Monk cried out in full voice for the first time, and he bent over the bones, touching the golden hair with a reverent hand.

I felt a hand on my shoulder but did not turn around, for as I watched, the golden skein of hair turned to dust under his fingers, one instant a braid and the next a reminder of time itself.

Brother Denneys threw himself onto the skeletons, weeping hysterically, and I — I flung myself down into the pit, though it was a drop of at least six feet. I pulled him off the brittle, broken bones and cradled him against me until his sorrow was spent. When I looked up, the grave was ringed around with the familiar faces of my brother monks. At the foot of the grave stood the abbot himself, his face as red and as angry as a wound.

Brother Denneys was sent away from Glastonbury, of course. He himself was a willing participant in the exile. For even though the little stone cross had the words HIC JACET ARTHURUS REX QUONDAM REXQUE FUTURUS carved upon it, he said it was not true. That the oak casket was nothing more than a boat from one of the lake villages overturned. That the hair we both saw so clearly in that early morning light was nothing more than grave mold.

"She is somewhere else, not here," he said, dismissing the torn earth with a wave of his hand. "And I must find her."

I followed him out the gate and down the road, keeping pace with him step for step. I follow him still. His hair has gotten grayer over the long years, a strand at a time, but cannot keep up with the script that now runs across my brow. The years as his squire have carved me deeply but his sorrowing face is untouched by time or the hundreds of small miracles he, all unknowing, brings with each opening of a grave: the girl in Westminster whose once blind eyes can now admit light, a Shropshire lad, dumb from birth, with a tongue that can now make rhymes.

And I understand that he will never find this particular grail. He is in his own hell and I but chart its regions, following after him on my two straight legs. A small miracle, true. In the winter, in the deepest snow, the right one pains me, a twisting memory of the old twisted bones. When I cry out in my sleep, he does not notice nor does he comfort me. And my ankle still warns of every coming storm. He is never grateful for the news. But I can walk for the most part without pain or limp, and surely every miracle maker needs a witness to his work, an apostle to send letters to the future. That is my burden. It is my duty. It is my everlasting joy.

The Tudor antiquary Bale reported that "In Avallon in 1191, there found they the flesh bothe of Arthur and of hys wyfe Guenever turned all into duste, wythin theyr coffines of strong oke, the boneys only remaynynge. A monke of the same abbeye, standyng and behouldyng the fine broydinges of the womman's hear as yellow as golde there still to remayne, as a man ravyshed, or more than halfe from his wyttes, he leaped into the graffe, xv fote depe, to have caughte them sodenlye. But he fayled of his purpose. For so soon as they were touched they fell all to powder."

By 1193, the monks at Glastonbury had money enough to work again on the rebuilding of their church, for wealthy pilgrims flocked to the relics and King Richard himself presented a sword reputed to be Excalibur to Tancred, the Norman ruler of Sicily, a few short months after the exhumation.

I was writing a series of fairy-tale-related poems and this one just popped out. Honest.

Toads

Sure, I called her *stupid cow*
and *witch*,
but only under my breath.
And I took an extra long lunch
last Friday,
and quit right at five
every day this week,
slapping my desk top down
with a noise
like the snap of gum.
She could've fired me right then.
Or docked my check.
Or put a pink slip
in my envelope
with that happy face
she draws on all her notes.
But not her.
Witch!
This morning
at the coffee shop,
when I went to order
a Danish and a decaf to go,
instead of words,
this great gray toad
the size of a bran muffin
dropped out between my lips
onto the Formica.

It looked up at me,
its dark eyes sorrowful,
its back marked
with Revlon's Lady Love
the shape of my kiss.
Tell me,
do you think
I should apologize?
Do you think I should let
the shop steward know?

I think of this story as Richard Gere meets Diana. Obviously I don't think much of either of them!

The Sleep of Trees

Never invoke the gods unless you really want them to appear. It annoys them very much.

— Chesterton

It had been a long winter. Arrhiza had counted every line and blister on the inside of the bark. Even the terrible binding power of the heartwood rings could not contain her longings. She desperately wanted spring to come so she could dance free, once again, of her tree. At night she looked up and through the spiky winter branches counted the shadows of early birds crossing the moon. She listened to the mewling of buds making their slow, painful passage to the light. She felt the sap veins pulse sluggishly around her. All the signs were there, spring was coming, spring was near, yet still there was no spring.

She knew that one morning, without warning, the rings would loosen and she would burst through the bark into her glade. It had happened every year of her life. But the painful wait, as winter slouched towards its dismal close, was becoming harder and harder to bear.

When Arrhiza had been younger, she had always slept the peaceful, uncaring sleep of trees. She would tumble, half-awake, through the bark and onto the soft, fuzzy green earth with the other young dryads, their arms and legs tangling in that first sleepy release. She had wondered then that the older trees released their burdens with such stately grace, the dryads and the meliades sending slow green praises into the air before the real Dance began. But she wondered no longer. Younglings simply slept the whole winter dreaming of what they knew best: roots and bark and the untroubling dark. But aging conferred knowledge, dreams change. Arrhiza now slept little and her waking, as her sleep, was filled with sky.

She even found herself dreaming of birds. Knowing trees were the honored daughters of the All Mother, allowed to root themselves deep into her flesh, knowing trees were the treasured sisters of the Huntress, allowed to unburden themselves into her sacred groves, Arrhiza envied birds. She wondered what it would be like to live apart from the land, to travel at will beyond the confines of the glade. Silly creatures though birds were, going from egg to earth without a thought, singing the same messages to one another throughout their short lives, Arrhiza longed to fly with one, passengered within its breast. A bird lived but a moment, but what a moment that must be.

Suddenly realizing her heresy, Arrhiza closed down her mind lest she share thoughts with her tree. She concentrated on the blessings to the All Mother and Huntress, turning her mind from sky to soil, from flight to the solidity of roots.

And in the middle of her prayer, Arrhiza fell out into spring, as surprised as if she were still young. She tumbled against one of the birch, her nearest neighbor, Phyla of the white face. Their legs touched, their hands brushing one another's thighs.

Arrhiza turned toward Phyla. "Spring comes late," she sighed, her breath caressing Phyla's budlike ear.

Phyla rolled away from her, pouting. "You make Spring Greeting sound like a complaint. It is the same every year." She sat up with her back to Arrhiza and stretched her arms. Her hands were outlined against the evening sky, the second and third fingers slotted together like a leaf. Then she turned slowly towards Arrhiza, her woodsgreen eyes unfocused. In the soft, filtered light her body gleamed whitely and the darker patches were mottled beauty marks on her breasts and sides. She was up to her feet in a single fluid movement and into the Dance.

Arrhiza watched, still full length on the ground, as one after another the dryads and meliades rose and stepped into position, circling, touching, embracing, moving apart. The cleft of their legs flashed pale signals around the glade.

Rooted to their trees, the hamadryads could only lean out into the Dance. They swayed to the lascivious pipings of spring. Their silver-green hair, thick as vines, eddied around their bodies like water.

Arrhiza watched it all but still did not move. How long she had waited for this moment, the whole of the deep winter, and yet she did not move. What she wanted was more than this, this entering into the Dance on command. She wanted to touch, to walk, to run, even to dance when she alone desired it. But then her blood was singing, her body pulsating; her limbs stretched upward answering the call. She was drawn towards the others and, even without willing it, Arrhiza was into the Dance.

Silver and green, green and gold, the grove was a smear of color and wind as she whirled around and around with her sisters. Who was touched and who the toucher; whose arm, whose thigh was pressed in the Dance, it did not matter. The Dance was all. Drops of perspiration, sticky as sap, bedewed their backs and ran slow rivulets to the ground. The Dance *was* the glade, *was* the grove. There was no stopping, no starting, for a circle has no beginning or end.

Then suddenly a hunter's horn knifed across the meadow. It was both discordant and sweet, sharp and caressing at once. The Dance did not stop but it dissolved. The Huntress was coming, the Huntress was here.

And then She was in the middle of them all, straddling a moon-beam, the red hem of Her saffron hunting tunic pulled up to expose muscled thighs. Seven hounds lay growling at Her feet. She reached up to Her hair and in one swift, savage movement pulled at the golden cords that bound it up. Her hair cascaded like silver and gold leaves onto Her shoulders and crept in tendrils across Her small, perfect breasts. Her heart-shaped face, with its crescent smile, was both innocent and corrupt; Her eyes as dark blue as a storm-coming sky. She dismounted the moon shaft and turned around slowly, as if displaying Herself to them all, but She was the Huntress, and She was doing the hunting. She looked into their faces one at a time, and the younger ones looked back, both eager and afraid.

Arrhiza was neither eager nor afraid. Twice already she had been the chosen one, torn laughing and screaming from the glade, brought for a night to the moon's dark side. The pattern of the Huntress' mouth was burned into her throat's hollow, Her mark, just as Her words were still in Arrhiza's ears. "You are mine. Forever. If you leave me, I will kill you, so fierce is my love." It had been spoken each time with a kind of passion, in between kisses, but the words, like the kisses, were as cold and distant and pitiless as the moon.

The Huntress walked around the circle once again, pausing longest before a young meliade, Pyrena of the apple blossoms. Under that gaze Pyrena seemed both to wither and to bloom. But the Huntress shook Her head and Her mouth formed the slightest moue of disdain. Her tongue flicked out and was caught momentarily between flawless teeth. Then She clicked to the hounds, who sprang up. Mounting the moon-beam again, She squeezed it with Her thighs and was gone, riding to another grove.

The moment She disappeared, the glade was filled with breathy gossip.

"Did you see…" began Dryope. Trembling with projected

pleasure, she turned to Pyrena. "The Huntress looked at you. Truly looked. Next time it *will* be you. I *know* it will."

Pyrena wound her fingers through her hair, letting fall a cascade of blossoms that perfumed the air. She shrugged but smiled a secret, satisfied smile.

Arrhiza turned abruptly and left the circle. She went back to her tree. Sluggishly the softened heartwood rings admitted her and she leaned into them, closed her eyes, and tried to sleep though she knew that in spring no true sleep would come.

She half-dreamed of clouds and birds, forcing them into her mind, but really she was hearing a buzzing. Sky, she murmured to herself, remember sky.

> "Oh trees, fair and flourishing, on the high hills They stand, lofty. The Deathless sacred grove…"

Jeansen practiced his Homeric supplication, intoning carefully through his nose. The words as they buzzed through his nasal passages tickled. He sneezed several times rapidly, a light punctuation to the verses. Then he continued:

> "…The Deathless sacred grove Men call them, and with iron never cut."

He could say the words perfectly now, his sounds rounded and full. The newly learned Greek rolled off his tongue. He had always been a fast study. Greek was his fifth language, if he counted Esperanto. He could even, on occasion, feel the meanings that hid behind the ancient poetry, but as often the meanings slid away, slippery little fish and he the incompetent angler.

He had come to Greece because he wanted to be known as

the American Olivier, the greatest classical actor the States had ever produced. He told interviewers he planned to learn Greek — classic Greek, not the Greek of the streets — to show them Oedipus from the amphitheaters where it had first been played. He would stand in the groves of Artemis, he had said, and call the Goddess to him in her own tongue. One columnist even suggested that with his looks and voice and reputation she would be crazy not to come. If she did, Jeansen thought to himself, smiling, I wouldn't treat her with any great distance. The goddesses like to play at shopgirls; the shopgirls, goddesses. And they all, he knew only too well, liked grand gestures.

And so he had traveled to Greece, not the storied isles of Homer but the fume-logged port of Piraeus, where a teacher with a mouthful of broken teeth and a breath only a harpy could love had taught him. But mouth and breath aside, he was a fine teacher and Jeansen a fine learner. Now he was ready. Artemis first, a special for PBS, and then the big movie. Oedipus starring *the* Jeansen Forbes.

Only right now all he could feel was the buzz of air, diaphragm against lungs, lungs to larynx, larynx to vocal chords, a mechanical vibration. Buzz, buzz, buzz.

He shook his head as if to clear it, and the well-cut blonde hair fell perfectly back in place. He reached a hand up to check it, then looked around the grove slowly, admiringly. The grass was long, uncut, but trampled down. The trees — he had not noticed it at first — were a strange mixture: birch and poplar, apple and oak. He was not a botanist, but it seemed highly unlikely that such a mix would have simply sprung up. Perhaps they had been planted years and years ago. *Note to himself, check on that.*

This particular grove was far up on Mount Cynthus, away from any roads and paths. He had stumbled on it by accident. Happy accident. But it was perfect, open enough for reenacting some of the supplicatory dances and songs, but the trees thick enough to add mystery. The guide book said that Cynthus had once been sacred to the Huntress, virgin Artemis, Diana of the moon. He liked that touch of authenticity. Perhaps her ancient worshippers had first seeded the glade. Even if he could not find the documentation, he could suggest it in such a way as to make it sound true enough.

Jeansen walked over to one birch, a young tree, slim and gracefully bending, He ran his hands down its white trunk. He rubbed a leaf between his fingers and considered the camera focusing on the action. He slowed the movement to a sensuous stroking. *Close up of hand and leaf, full frame.*

Next to the birch was an apple, so full of blossoms there was a small fall of petals puddling the ground. He pushed them about tentatively with his boot. Even without wind, more petals drifted from the tree to the ground. *Long tracking shot as narrator kicks through the pile of white flowers, lap dissolve to a single blossom.*

Standing back from the birch and the apple tree, tall and unbending, was a mature oak. It looked as if it were trying to keep the others from getting close. Its reluctance to enter the circle of trees made Jeansen move over to it. Then he smiled at his own fancies. He was often, he knew, too fanciful, yet such invention was also one of his great strengths as an actor. He took off his knapsack and set it down at the foot of the oak like an offering. Then he turned and leaned against the tree, scratching between his shoulder blades with the rough bark. *Long shot of man in grove, move in slowly for tight close-up. Voice over.*

"But when the fate of death is drawing near,
First wither on the earth the beauteous trees,
The bark around them wastes, the branches

fall, And the Nymph's soul, at the same moment, leaves The sun's fair light."

He let two tears funnel down his cheeks. Crying was easy. He
could call upon tears whenever he wanted to, even before a
word was spoken in a scene. They meant nothing anymore.
Extremely tight shot on tear, then slow dissolve to…

A hand touched his face, reaching around him from behind.
Startled, Jeansen grabbed at the arm, held, and turned.

"Why do you water your face?"

He stared. It was a girl, scarcely in her teens, with the
clearest complexion he had ever seen and flawless features,
except for a crescent scar at her throat which somehow made
the rest more perfect. His experienced eyes traveled quickly
down her body. She was naked under a light green chiffon shift.
He wondered where they had gotten her, what she wanted. A
part in the special?

"Why do you water your face?" she asked again. Then this
time she added, "You are a man." It was almost a question. She
moved around before him and knelt unself-consciously.

Jeansen suddenly realized she was speaking ancient Greek.
He had thought her English with that skin. But the hair was
black with blue-green highlights. Perhaps she *was* Greek.

He held her face in his hands and tilted it up so that she met
him eye to eye. The green of her eyes was unbelievable. He
thought they might be lenses, but saw no telltale double
impression in the eye.

Jeansen chose his words with care, but first he smiled, the
famous slow smile printed on posters and magazine covers.
"You," he said, pronouncing the Greek with gentle precision,
his voice carefully low and tremulous, "you are a goddess."

She leaped up and drew back, holding her hands before her.
"No, no," she cried, her voice and body registering such fear

that Jeansen rejected it at once. This was to be a classic play, not a horror flick.

But even if she couldn't act, she was damned beautiful. He closed his eyes for a moment, imprinting her face on his memory. And he thought for a moment of her pose, the hands held up. There had been something strange about them. She had too many — or too few — fingers. He opened his eyes to check them, and she was gone.

"Damned bit players," he muttered at last, angry to have wasted so much time on her. He took the light tent from his pack and set it up. Then he went to gather sticks for a fire. It could get pretty cold in the mountains in early spring, or so he had been warned.

From the shelter of the tree, Arrhiza watched the man. He moved gracefully, turning, gesturing, stooping. His voice was low and full of music and he spoke the prayers with great force. Why had she been warned that men were coarse, unfeeling creatures? He was far more beautiful than any of the worshippers who came cautiously at dawn in their black-beetle dresses, creeping down the paths like great nicophorus from the hidden chambers of earth, to lift their year-scarred faces to the sky. They brought only jars of milk, honey, and oil, but he came bringing a kind of springy joy. And had he not wept when speaking of the death of trees, the streams from his eyes as crystal as any that ran near the grove? Clearly this man was neither coarse nor unfeeling.

A small breeze stirred the top branches, and Arrhiza glanced up for a moment, but even the sky could not hold her interest today. She looked back at the stranger, who was pulling oddments from his pack. He pounded small nails into the earth, wounding it with every blow, yet did not fear its cries.

Arrhiza was shocked. What could he be doing? Then she

realized he was erecting a dwelling of some kind. It was unthinkable — yet this stranger had thought it. No votary would dare stay in a sacred grove past sunfall, dare carve up the soil on which the trees of the Huntress grew. To even think of being near when the Dance began was a desecration. And to see the Huntress, should She visit this glade at moonrise, was to invite death. Arrhiza shivered. She was well-schooled in the history of Actaeon, torn by his own dogs for the crime of spying upon Her.

Yet this man was unafraid. As he worked, he raised his voice — speaking, laughing, weeping, singing. He touched the trees with bold, unshaking hands. It was the trees, not the man, who trembled at his touch. Arrhiza shivered again, remembering the feel of him against the bark, the muscles hard under the fabric of his shirt. Not even the Huntress had such a back.

Then perhaps, she considered, this fearless votary was not a man at all. Perhaps he was a god come down to tease her, test her, take her by guile or by force. Suddenly, she longed to be wooed.

"You are a goddess," he had said. And it had frightened her. Yet only a god would dare such a statement. Only a god, such as Eros, might take time to woo. She would wait and let the night reveal him. If he remained untouched by the Huntress and unafraid, she would know.

Jeansen stood in front of the tent and watched the sun go down. It seemed to drown itself in blood, the sky bathed in an elemental red that was only slowly leeched out. Evening, however, was an uninteresting entr'acte. He stirred the coals on his campfire and climbed into the tent. *Lap dissolve...*

Lying in the dark, an hour later, still sleepless, he thought about the night. He often went camping by himself in the California mountains, away from the telephone and his fans.

Intercut other campsites. He knew enough to carry a weapon against marauding mountain lions or curious bears. But the silence of this Greek night was more disturbing than all the snufflings and howlings in the American dark. He had never heard anything so complete before — no crickets, no wind, no creaking of trees.

He turned restlessly and was surprised to see that the tent side facing the grove was backlit by some kind of diffused lighting. Perhaps it was the moon. It had become a screen, and shadow women seemed to dance across it in patterned friezes. It had to be a trick of his imagination, trees casting silhouettes. Yet without wind, how did they move?

As he watched, the figures came more and more into focus, clearly women. This was no trick of imagination, but of human proposing. If it was one of the columnists or some of his erstwhile friends... Try to frighten him, would they? He would give them a good scare instead.

He slipped into his khaki shorts and found the pistol in his pack. Moving stealthily, he stuck his head out of the tent. And froze.

Instead of the expected projector, he saw real women dancing, silently beating out a strange exotic rhythm. They touched, stepped, circled. There was no music that he could hear, yet not one of them misstepped. And each was as lovely as the girl he had met in the grove.

Jeansen wondered briefly if they were local girls hired for an evening's work. But they were each so incredibly beautiful, it seemed unlikely they could all be from any one area. Then suddenly realizing it didn't matter, that he could simply watch and enjoy it, Jeansen chuckled to himself. It was the only sound in the clearing. He settled back on his haunches and smiled.

The moon rose slowly as if reluctant to gain the sky. Arrhiza watched it silver the landscape. Tied to its rising, she was pulled into the Dance.

Yet as she danced a part of her rested still within the tree, watching. And she wondered. Always before, without willing it, she was wholly a part of the Dance. Whirling, stepping along with the other dryads, their arms, her arms; their legs, her legs. But now she felt as cleft as a tree struck by a bolt. The watching part of her trembled in anticipation.

Would the man emerge from his hasty dwelling? Would he prove himself a god? She watched and yet she dared not watch, each turn begun and ended with the thought, the fear.

And then his head appeared between the two curtains of his house, his bare shoulders, his bronzed and muscled chest. His face registered first a kind of surprise, then a kind of wonder, and at last delight. There was no fear. He laughed and his laugh was more powerful than the moon. It drew her to him and she danced slowly before her god.

Setting; moon-lit glade. 30–35 girls dancing. No Busby Berkeley kicklines, please. Try for a frenzied yet sensuous native dance. Robbins? Sharp? Ailey? Absolutely no dirndls. Light make-up. No spots. Diffused light. Music: an insistent pounding, feet on grass. Maybe a wild piping. Wide shot of entire dance then lap dissolve to single dancer. She begins to slow down, dizzy with anticipation, dread. Her god has chosen her…

Jeansen stood up as one girl turned slowly around in front of him and held out her arms. He leaned forward and caught her up, drew her to him.

A god is different, thought Arrhiza, as she fell into his arms. They tumbled onto the fragrant grass.

He was soft where the Huntress was hard, hard where She was soft. His smell was sharp, of earth and mold; Hers was musk and air.

"Don't leave," he whispered, though Arrhiza had made no movement to go. "I swear I'll kill myself if you leave." He pulled her gently into the canvas dwelling.

She went willingly though she knew that a god would say no such thing. Yet knowing he was but a man, she stayed and opened herself under him, drew him in, felt him shudder above her, then heavily fall. There was thunder outside the dwelling and the sound of dogs growling. Arrhiza heard it all and, hearing, did not care. The Dance outside had ended abruptly. She breathed gently in his ear, "It is done."

He grunted his acceptance and rolled over onto his side, staring at nothing but a hero's smile playing across his face. Arrhiza put her hand over his mouth to silence him and he brought up his hand to hers. He counted the fingers with his own and sighed. It was then that the lightning struck, breaking her tree, her home, her heart, her life.

She was easy, Jeansen thought. Beautiful and silent and easy, the best sort of woman. He smiled into the dark. He was still smiling when the tree fell across the tent, bringing the canvas down around them and crushing three of his ribs. A spiky branch pierced his neck, ripping the larynx. He pulled it out frantically and tried to scream, tried to breathe. A ragged hissing of air through the hole was all that came out. He reached for the girl and fainted.

Three old women in black dresses found him in the morning. They pushed the tree off the tent, off Jeansen, and half carried, half dragged him down the mountainside. They found no girl.

He would live, the doctor said through gold and plaster teeth, smiling proudly.

Live. Jeansen turned the word over in his mind, bitterer

than any tears. In Greek or in English, the word meant little to him now. *Live.* His handsome face unmarred by the fallen tree seemed to crack apart with the effort to keep from crying. He shaped the word with his lips but no sound passed them. Those beautiful, melodious words would never come again. His voice had leaked out of his neck with his blood.

Camera moves in silently for a tight close-up. Only sounds are routine hospital noises; and mounting over them to an overpowering cacophony is a steady, harsh, rasping breathing, as credits roll.

I wrote this poem when I was in my twenties. This is the one Adam set to music and the band performed. Go figure.

Prince Charming Comes

The goose flies past the setting sun, plums roasting in her breast;
Sleeping Beauty lays her head a hundred years to rest.
Then fee, fi, fo the giant fums
And to my dark Prince Charming comes
A ride, a ride, a ride, a riding,
Into my night of darkness, my own Prince Charming comes.

The witch is popped into the oven, rising into cake;
The swan queen glides her downy form to the enchanted lake.
And rum-pum-pum the drummer drums
As into darkness my love comes
A ride, a ride, a ride, a riding,
Into my night of darkness, my own Prince Charming comes.

But do you come to take me out
Or come to put me in?
But do you come to yield to me
Or do you come to win?

It's half past twelve and once again the shoe of glass is gone,
And magic is as magic was and vanished with the dawn.
For Pooh has hummed his final hums,
The giant finished off his fums,
                              they've drawn their final breath.
For into darkness my prince comes
A ride, a ride, a ride, a riding,
For into darkness my prince comes
On his bony horse called death.

MERLE
INYINGA
1991

This is one of three stories about The Shouting Fey, a family of fairies I absolutely love. The other two stories are "The Thirteenth Fey," which is a redaction of the Sleeping Beauty mythos, and "Dusty Loves," which wreaks a peculiar havoc on Romeo and Juliet. This one doesn't play entirely nice-nice with the church, but since when do writers have to play by the rules? Some day, when the time fairy (a fourth cousin of Finn's, I am sure) leaves enough time around my house, I want to write about a half dozen more stories about this family and get the book published as a whole.

The Uncorking of Uncle Finn

Uncle Finn had angered the Abbot. It had something to do with blasphemy — the Abbot's, not Uncle Finn's. Uncle had been converted several centuries before by the Irish saint Patrick and was deeply religious still, given to falling on his knees in the unlikeliest of places: rookeries, backstairs, tidal pools, butter churns. The Abbot, on the other hand, was a pagan and a drunk besides. It was inevitable that the two should clash over matters of faith.

Now I grant you that it is unnerving for the locals to have a fanatically Christianized elf forever exhorting them to es-chew evil and seek the good, popping up unexpectedly in their most secret places of vice. He knew where every still was working, every mistress kept, every bit of falsified paper stored. He had a nose for venialness. But as he had been proselytizing for more than three centuries in his own curious way, one would have thought the humans would have grown used to it. And indeed, those who could stand it the least had long since left, moving to Killarney or Glocamorra or catching a ride with itinerant saints, sailing westward over the treacherous seas in coracles made of glass. There were some just that desperate to escape Uncle Finn's exhortations.

The Abbot, however, was newly appointed, being a sinner of great renown on the Continent. It was thought by the bishop that a year of two in Kilkenny under the watchful eye of Uncle Finn would wear him down. It was the bishop's own version of a finishing school, and he was prepared to finish the Abbot or kill him in the process.

The war had begun as soon as the Abbot had set foot in the cellar, that being Uncle Finn's province. He was partial to dark places; his maternal great-grandmother had once lived with a troll, and Finn took after that side.

The Abbot's first trip to the cellar was without warning. He had disconnected the bell that rang over the cellarer's head, a precaution even his most fervid detractors had applauded. That way, of course, no one could count the number of times he visited belowstairs. Kilkenny Abbey was well known not only for its wines and a surprisingly good claret, but also for its hardier brews: kümmel made with an imported caraway seed, a plum drink concocted with the help of a recipe lent by the Slovakian saint Slivos, and a wild blackthorn gin that had been said to rock even the toughest of European soldiery.

To say Uncle Finn was surprised by the Abbot is an understatement. He was astonished out of three Hail Marys. They bled from his lips and lost him the conversion of three recalcitrant mice and a reprobate rat.

One must also imagine the Abbot's astonishment, for no one had warned him about Uncle Finn. He had come tripping down the stairs, ready for further lubrication, and suddenly there was this wee attenuated creature garbed in green on knobby knees before a congregation of reluctant rodents. Is it any wonder the Abbot cried out and held his head? Or that Uncle Finn reciprocated with the bloody Hail Marys and an elvish curse that shattered three bottles of the best claret that the Abbot had hoped to save for after midnight Mass?

The Abbot fired the second shot of the war, a letter to the pope requesting excommunication for all faerie folk on the grounds that everyone knew that they had no souls. But the pope refused the request, for he himself had once held similar views when he was but a seminarian. And then he had pronounced that his walking stick would sooner grow blossoms than a certain nixie of the local pond might enter heaven. He had not known she was a convert, one of the magdalens brought round by a recent crusade. No sooner had the words been out of his mouth, than his staff had sprouted a feathering of ferns and spatulate leaves and begun to bud. So the pope was not about to deny the possibility of souls to any of the Good Folk. In effect, he left the matter entirely in the bishop's hands.

This so displeased the Abbot, he turned his displeasure into a monumental drunk using the sacramental wine, a drunk that ended only when he awoke in his cell the Sunday before Lent to see Uncle Finn perched on his bedfoot, hands upraised, the spirit of the Lord and all the Irish saints moving in his mouth.

"Arise," cried Uncle Finn, "and go forth."

The Abbot arose, and his sandal went forth and smacked Uncle Finn right between the eyes while all the while the Abbot praised the Lord.

Now a sandal and Uncle Finn are about the same size, so there was more damage than either the Abbot or the Good Lord intended. So the Abbot was, indeed, forced to arise and scoop up Uncle Finn's body from the stone floor. He brought Uncle Finn, wrapped in a linen handkerchief, to the infirmarer, a certain Brother Elias.

"What can you do with this thing?" asked the Abbot. However, as he was holding Uncle Finn wrapped in the handkerchief in his left hand and his right was holding his own head (and it still ringing from the three days of steady drinking), it was no wonder Brother Elias's answer was confusing.

"If you'd stop bending your elbow, my lord Abbot," said the old monk, "your head would be marvelously improved. It's a wonder of anatomy, it is, that head and elbow are so connected." The infirmarer, being a reformed tippler himself, had plenty more salvos where that one came from. He had given up drink and taken up religion with the same fervor.

"Not my elbow and not my head, you Kilkenny clodpate! This!" The Abbot held out his left hand, where, in the linen, Uncle Finn was just coming to.

"Saints in heaven, but it's Finn," cried Elias, making the sign of the cross hastily and missing a fourth of it.

"That's not fine at all," said the Abbot, who had no tolerance for any accents save his own.

"Not fine, Finn," explained the infirmarer, but since he pronounced them the same, it led to a few more moments of misunderstanding until he reached over and gently removed Uncle Finn from his winding sheet. "You had better be asking his pardon, my lord. He's a Christian now for sure, which means he will turn the other cheek as often as not. But he's still quite a hand at elvish curses when he's riled. Better not to be on his bad side."

"He's already on *my* bad side." roared the Abbot, remembering with renewed fury the three bottles of claret. "Fix him up, tidy him up, and shut him up. Then report to me. The minute he can handle a good strong talking-to, I want to know."

But Finn was already beginning to sit up, and reaching his wee hands up to his wee head. What was not clear to the two monks was that Finn, while awake, was not aware. The sandal had quite addled him. His magic was turned around and about widdershins. He began to moan and speak in tongues.

"Oh, for Our Lord's sake," cried the Abbot with great

feeling, his own head twanging like a tuning fork by the tone of those tongues.

The supplication to Our Lord brought Uncle Finn's eyes wide open, and he began to sing hosannas.

"I wish he'd put a cork in it!" cried the Abbot, his hands to his ears.

At the word *wish*, Finn's eyes got a strange glow in them, and everything not human in the room began to stir about as if caught up in a twisting wind. Faster and faster anything not pinned down began to move: glasses and retorts; bunches of drying patience, pepperwort, and clary; mortars and pestles; long lines of linen bandages; copies of *Popular Errors in Physick*, Mithradates' receipt for *Venice Treacle*, and Drayton's *Hermit*. All the while, Uncle Finn kept chanting:

> *Pickles and peas, knife and fork,*
> *Find a bottle, carve a cork,*
> *Wind it up and in the wine*
> *A sailor's life is mighty fine.*

Which, of course, is a terribly mixed-up version of the old bottle spell used mostly by drunken mages to call up spirits.

Sea winds began to blow, spouts of whales were sighted, dolphin clicks heard, and with one last incredible *whoooosh*, the whole of the whirling stuff was sucked in through the neck of a nearby bottle of Bordeaux '79 that Elias used for medicinal purposes only, it being too sour and full of sediment for a tippler of taste. The displaced wine splattered all over the infirmary, and the room smelled like a pothouse for a week.

Then, with a final *thwap*, the cork replaced itself. The stirring continued inside the bottle for fully a minute more, and when the wind and mist and moisture had resolved itself, there appeared inside the light green bottle a passable imitation of a sailing ship, with a pestle for a mainmast and linen bandages for sails. Clinging to the mortar steering wheel was Uncle Finn, looking both puzzled and pleased. He gave a weak smile in the direction of the cork, put his hand on his head, and slid down in a faint onto the papier-mâché deck on which the ingredients for *Venice Treacle* could still be discerned.

"Oh, my Lord," said the infirmarer, not really sure if he meant the salutation to have a capital *L* or a small one.

But the Abbot, taking it was himself addressed, said softly, "And *that* should do it."

For a week he was right, for the abbey was quiet and filled with plainsong laced only with the Abbot's own version of an old capstan chanty sung fully a half note off-tune.

But the communications of the Fey, while sometimes slow, are sure. The rodent proselytes told their families, one of whose members was overheard by a wandering and early June bug. The June bug's connections included a will-o'-the-wisp who had married into Uncle Finn's family. It was scarcely a week later that word of Uncle Finn's incarceration came to my father's ears.

By the time he had sorted through his meager store of magicks and translated himself to the far side of the island, using a map in one of his books that was sadly too many years ahead of its time, twelve boggles, banshees, nuggles, and a ghost (all relatives) had been to visit before him. The abbey had, in that short week's time, gotten itself a reputation for being haunted — as indeed it was, in a manner of speaking — and the humans had summarily deserted the abbey grounds until the proper exorcists might be found.

None of this, of course, helped poor Uncle Finn. No one but a human could pull the cork from the Bordeaux bottle, for it had been placed there by a human wish. And as long as the visits continued, no human would venture near the place.

My father sighed and stared at his brother, whom he remembered fondly as an elf of high promise and a great sense of humor. Uncle Finn looked little like the memory, being sadly faded and a bit green, a property not only of the tinted glass but of his initial handling, seasickness, and a week corked up in a bottle that still reeked of wine.

Father shouted at him and Finn shouted back, but their voices were strained through the layers of green glass. Conversation was impossible. At last Father came home, whey-faced and desperate-looking. In fact, all the relatives had left, for there was nothing any of them could do except sigh. As the last of them departed, the priestly exorcists arrived. Humans have this marvelous ability to time their exits and entrances, which is why they — and not the Fey — hold theatrical events. They spoke their magic words and threw about a great deal of incense and believed that it was their own efforts that rid the abbey of the Fey. But like a plumber who gets paid after a sink has fixed itself, they were praised for nothing. Visiting Fey never overstay their welcome nor hang about when nothing can be done. It is simply not in our nature.

The Abbot had, of course, sworn Elias to secrecy concerning Uncle Finn and the bottle, and the two of them had replaced the Bordeaux '79 on the wine cellar racks without the cellarer's knowledge. But Elias, after a week in a room smelling strongly of tipple, returned to his old ways, and after that his vow of secrecy mattered little, for no one would have believed a word he had to say. As for the Abbot, after a year of the most flagrant misrule, he was sent by the pope on a crusade against the infidels from which he did not return, though there were frequent rumors that he had become a sheikh in a distant emirate and had banned all peris and djinn from his borders.

That left Uncle Finn corked up in his bottle on a back shelf in a cellar of a once-haunted Abbey, marked as a wine so degraded and unpopular that it would never be taken by any knowledgeable person from the shelf. And we were afraid he would remain so forever.

But one day, as I sat reading in my father's library, which is well stocked with books of the past, present, and future, I came upon a volume in section A. A for Archaeology, Astronomy, Ancestry, and Aphorisms. It was a splendid piece of serendipity, for the book told about the Americas, where, in some distant year, a man rich in coins but lacking in wisdom would take Kilkenny Abbey stone by stone over the great waters, a feat even a Merlin might envy. And — as one of the Aphorists wrote in another volume in that section, since Americans would have no wine before its time — surely the magical words "Bordeaux '79" will reek of such time. Uncle Finn, oh Uncle Finn, you will have before you an entire continent to convert, and proselytes beyond counting, for a land that saves its saviors in plaster and seeds the heavens with saucers should have no trouble at all accepting a bottle saint.

This is a true family story, which in Yolen terms may be an oxymoron. It's said that my grandmother went mad for several years after the death of those children. Then one day she gave birth to twins — my aunts Eva and Sylvia — and felt God had given her back her life. She was sane thereafter. So sane, in fact, that she was called "The General" by her children.

Smallpox

My grandmother lay down
in her Russian bed,
two children at her breast,
one child at her back,
and one curled, doglike, at her feet,
all touched by fire
and the calculus of pain.
They lay in their sweat
like herrings in brine.
Ykaterinislav,
Ykaterinislav,
who mourns the children,
who calculates their loss,
the village so halved,
it was beyond crying.
She lay down with four,
arose with one.
How could she get up,
knowing God's casual mathematics,
the subtraction that so divided
her uncountable heart.

At a writer's conference I met a woman with one leg who had recently lost so much weight, she was positively anorexic. She told me that her mother was a concentration camp survivor. When I asked her what her mother thought of her weight loss, she replied without a trace of self-awareness or irony: "She thinks I look like someone from the camps." It was the start of this story, the first draft of which I finished at the conference. The story bounced from all the major literary and sf/fantasy magazines, always with wonderful notes. My favorite was from Ed Ferman at F&SF, who wrote that of the two stories I had sent him, "Names" was the better, possibly the best story I had ever written, but it wasn't for him. He was buying the other. I put "Names" in my collection Tales of Wonder *and it was chosen for one of the stories in Karl Edward Wagner's* Year's Best Horror *anthologies. Go figure.*

Names

Her mother's number had been D248960. It was still imprinted on her arm, burned into the flesh, a permanent journal entry. Rachel had heard the stories, recited over and over in the deadly monotone her mother took on to tell of the camp. Usually her mother had a beautiful voice, low, musical. Men admired it. Yet not a month went by that something was not said or read or heard that reminded her, and she began reciting the names, last names, in order, in a sepulchral accent:

ABRAHMS
BERLINER
BRODSKY
DANNENBERG
FISCHER

FRANK
GLASSHEIM
GOLDBLATT

It was her one party trick, that recitation. But Rachel always knew that when the roll call was done, her mother would start the death-camp stories. Whether the audience wanted to hear them or not, she would surround them with their own guilt and besiege them with the tales:

HEGELMAN
ISAACS
KAPLAN
KOHN

Her mother had been a child in the camp; had gone through puberty there; had left with her life. Had been lucky. The roll call was of the dead ones, the unlucky ones. The children in the camp had each been imprinted with a portion of the names, a living y*ahrzeit*, little speaking candles; their eyes burning, their flesh burning, wax in the hands of the adults who had told them: "You must remember. If you do not remember, we never lived. If you do not remember, we never died." And so they remembered.

Rachel wondered if, all over the world, there were survivors, men and women who, like her mother, could recite those names:

LEVITZ
MAMOROWITZ
MORGENSTERN
NORENBERG
ORENSTEIN

REESE

Some nights she dreamed of them: hundreds of old children, wizened toddlers, marching toward her, their arms over their heads to show the glowing numbers, reciting names.

ROSENBLUM
ROSENWASSER
SOLOMON
STEIN

It was an epic poem, those names, a ballad in alphabetics. Rachel could have recited them along with her mother, but her mouth never moved. It was an incantation. Hear, O Israel, Germany, America. The names had an awful power over her, and even in her dreams she could not speak them aloud. The stories of the camps, of the choosing of victims — left line to the ovens, right to another day of deadening life — did not frighten her. She could move away from the group that listened to her mother's tales. There was no magic in the words that told of mutilations, of children's brains against the Nazi walls. She could choose to listen or not listen; such recitations did not paralyze her. But the names:

TANNENBAUM
TEITLEMAN
VANNENBERG
WASSERMAN
WECHTENSTEIN
ZEISS

Rachel knew that the names had been spoken at the moment of her birth: that her mother, legs spread, the waves of

Rachel's passage rolling down her stomach, had breathed the names between spasms long before Rachel's own name had been pronounced. Rachel Rebecca Zuckerman. That final *Zeiss* had burst from her mother's lips as Rachel had slipped out, greasy with birth blood. Rachel knew she had heard the names in the womb. They had opened the uterine neck, they had lured her out and beached her as easily as a fish. How often had her mother commented that Rachel had never cried as a child. Not once. Not even at birth when the doctor had slapped her. She knew, even if her mother did not, that she had been silenced by the incantation, the *Zeiss* a stopper in her mouth.

When Rachel was a child, she had learned the names as another child would a nursery rhyme. The rhythm of the passing syllables was as water in her mouth, no more than nonsense words. But at five, beginning to understand the power of the names, she could say them no more. For the saying was not enough. It did not satisfy her mother's needs. Rachel knew that there was something more she needed to do to make her mother smile.

At thirteen, on her birthday, she began menstruating, and her mother watched her get dressed. "So plump. So *zaftik*." It was an observation, less personal than a weather report. But she knew it meant that her mother had finally seen her as more than an extension, more than a child still red and white from its passage into the light.

It seemed that, all at once, she knew what to do. Her mother's duty had been the Word. Rachel's was to be the Word Made Flesh.

She stopped eating.

The first month, fifteen pounds poured off her. Melted. Ran as easily as candle wax. She thought only of food. Bouillon. Lettuce. Carrots. Eggs. Her own private poem. What she missed most was chewing. In the camp they chewed on gristle and wood. It was one of her mother's best tales.

The second month her cheekbones emerged, sharp reminders of the skull. She watched the mirror and prayed. *Barukh atah adonai elohenu melekh ha-olam*. She would not say the words for bread or wine. Too many calories. Too many pounds. She cut a star out of yellow posterboard and held it to her breast. The face in the mirror smiled back. She rushed to the bathroom and vomited away another few pounds. When she flushed the toilet, the sound was a hiss, as if gas were escaping into the room.

The third month she discovered laxatives, and the names on the containers became an addition to her litany: Metamucil, Agoral, Senokot. She could feel the chair impress itself on her bones. Bone on wood. If it hurt to sit, she would lie down.

She opened her eyes and saw the ceiling, spread above her like a sanitized sky. A voice pronounced her name. "Rachel, Rachel Zuckerman. Answer me."

But no words came out. She raised her right hand, a signal; she was weaker than she thought. Her mother's face, smiling, appeared. The room was full of cries. There was a chill in the air, damp, crowded. The smell of decay was sweet and beckoning. She closed her eyes and the familiar chant began, and Rachel added her voice to the rest. It grew stronger near the end:

ABRAHMS
BERLINER
BRODSKY
DANNENBERG
FISCHER
FRANK
GLASSHEIM
GOLDBLATT

HEGELMAN
ISAACS
KAPLAN
KOHN
LEVITZ
MAMOROWITZ
MORGENSTERN
NORENBERG
ORENSTEIN
REESE
ROSENBLUM
ROSENWASSER
SOLOMON
STEIN
TANNENBAUM
TEITLEMAN
VANNENBERG
WASSERMAN
WECHTENSTEIN
ZEISS
ZUCKERMAN

They said the final name together and then, with a little sputter, like a *yahrzeit* candle at the end, she went out.

This is what happens when a writer simultaneously takes a Victorian Children's Literature course and a course in folklore. Wires cross and suddenly George MacDonald's grandmother from The Princess and the Goblin *is mixed up with the term paper on Cinderella variants!*

The Moon Ribbon

There was once a plain but good-hearted girl named Sylva whose sole possession was a ribbon her mother had left her. It was a strange ribbon, the color of moonlight, for it had been woven from the gray hairs of her mother and her mother's mother and her mother's mother's mother before her.

Sylva lived with her widowed father in a great house by the forest's edge. Once the great house had belonged to her mother, but when she died, it became Sylva's father's house to do with as he willed. And what he willed was to live simply and happily with his daughter without thinking of the day to come.

But one day, when there was little enough to live on, and only the great house to recommend him, Sylva's father married again, a beautiful widow who had two beautiful daughters of her own.

It was a disastrous choice, for no sooner were they wed when it was apparent the woman was mean in spirit and meaner in tongue. She dismissed most of the servants and gave their chores over to Sylva, who followed her orders without complaint. For simply living in her mother's house with her loving father seemed enough for the girl.

After a bit, however, the old man died in order to have some peace, and the house passed on to the stepmother. Scarcely two days had passed, or maybe three, when the stepmother left off mourning the old man and turned on Sylva. She dismissed the last of the servants without their pay.

"Girl," she called out, for she never used Sylva's name, "you will sleep in the kitchen and do the charring." And from that time on it was so.

Sylva swept the floor and washed and mended the family's clothing. She sowed and hoed and tended the fields. She ground the wheat and kneaded the bread, and she waited on the others as though she were a servant. But she did not complain.

Yet late at night, when the stepmother and her own two daughters were asleep, Sylva would weep bitterly into her pillow, which was nothing more than an old broom laid in front of the hearth.

One day, when she was cleaning out an old desk, Sylva came upon a hidden drawer she had never seen before. Trembling, she opened the drawer. It was empty except for a silver ribbon with a label attached to it. *For Sylva* read the card. *The Moon Ribbon of Her Mother's Hair.* She took it out and stared at it. And all that she had lost was borne in upon her. She felt the tears start in her eyes, and so as not to cry she took the tag off and began to stroke the ribbon with her hand. It was rough and smooth at once and shone like the rays of the moon.

At that moment her stepsisters came into the room.

"What is that?" asked one. "Is it nice? It is mine."

"I want it. I saw it first," cried the other.

The noise brought the stepmother to them. "Show it to me," she said.

Obediently, Sylva came over and held the ribbon out to her. But when the stepmother picked it up, it looked like no more than strands of gray hair woven together unevenly. It was prickly to the touch.

"Disgusting," said the stepmother, dropping it back into

Sylva's hand. "Throw it out at once."

"Burn it," cried one stepsister.

"Bury it," cried the other.

"Oh, please. It was my mother's. She left it for me. Please let me keep it," begged Sylva.

The stepmother looked again at the gray strand. "Very well," she said with a grim smile. "It suits you." And she strode out of the room, her daughters behind her.

Now that she had the silver ribbon, Sylvia thought her life would be better. But instead it became worse. As if to punish her for speaking out for the ribbon, her sisters were at her to wait on them both day and night. And whereas before she had to sleep by the hearth, she now had to sleep outside with the animals. Yet she did not complain or run away, for she was tied by her memories to her mother's house.

One night, when the frost was on the grass turning each blade into a silver spear, Sylva threw herself to the ground in tears. And the silver ribbon, which she had tied loosely about her hair, slipped off and lay on the ground before her. She had never seen it in the moonlight. It glittered and shone and seemed to ripple.

Sylva bent over to touch it and her tears fell upon it. Suddenly the ribbon began to grow and change, and as it changed the air was filled with a woman's soft voice speaking these words:

> *Silver ribbon, silver hair,*
> *Carry Sylva with great care,*
> *Bring my daughter home.*

And there at Sylva's feet was a silver river that glittered and shone and rippled in the moonlight.

There was neither boat nor bridge, but Sylva did not care. She thought the river would wash away her sorrows, and without a single word, she threw herself in.

But she did not sink. Instead she floated like a swan and the river bore her on, on past houses and hills, past high places and low. And strange to say, she was not wet at all.

At last she was carried around a great bend in the river and deposited gently on a grassy slope that came right down to the water's edge. Sylva scrambled up onto the bank and looked about. There was a great meadow of grass so green and still it might have been painted on. At the meadow's rim, near a dark forest, sat a house that was like and yet not like the one in which Sylva lived.

"Surely someone will be there who can tell me where I am and why I have been brought here," she thought. So she made her way across the meadow and only where she stepped down did the grass move. When she moved beyond, the grass sprang back and was the same as before. And though she passed larkspur and meadowsweet, clover and rye, they did not seem like real flowers, for they had no smell at all.

"Am I dreaming?" she wondered, "or am I dead?" But she did not say it out loud, for she was afraid to speak into the silence.

Sylva walked up to the house and hesitated at the door. She feared to knock and yet feared equally not to. As she was deciding, the door opened of itself and she walked in.

She found herself in a large, long, dark hall with a single crystal door at the end that emitted a strange glow the color of moonlight. As she walked down the hall, her shoes made no clatter on the polished wood floor. And when she reached the door, she tried to peer through into the room beyond, but the crystal panes merely gave back her own reflection twelve times.

Sylva reached for the doorknob and pulled sharply. The glowing crystal knob came off in her hand. She would have wept then, but anger stayed her; she beat her fist against the door and it suddenly gave way.

Inside was a small room lit only by a fireplace and a round white globe that hung from the ceiling like a pale, wan moon. Before the fireplace stood a tall woman dressed all in white. Her silver-white hair was unbound and cascaded to her knees. Around her neck was a silver ribbon.

"Welcome, my daughter," she said.

"Are you my mother?" asked Sylva wonderingly, for what little she remembered of her mother, she remembered no one as grand as this.

"I am if you make me so," came the reply.

"And how do I do that?" asked Sylva.

"Give me your hand."

As the woman spoke, she seemed to move away, yet she moved not at all. Instead the floor between them moved and cracked apart. Soon they were separated by a great chasm which was so black it seemed to have no bottom.

"I cannot reach," said Sylva.

"You must try," the woman replied.

So Sylva clutched the crystal knob to her breast and leaped, but it was too far. As she fell, she heard a woman's voice speaking from behind her and before her and all about her, warm with praise.

"Well done, my daughter. You are halfway home."

Sylva landed gently on the meadow grass, but a moment's walk from her house. In her hand she still held the knob, shrunk now to the size of a jewel. The river shimmered once before her and was gone, and where it had been was the silver ribbon, lying limp and damp in the morning frost.

The door to the house stood open. She drew a deep breath and went in.

"What is that?" cried one of the stepsisters when she saw the crystalline jewel in Sylva's hand.

"I want it," cried the other, grabbing it from her.

"I will take that," said the stepmother, snatching it from them all. She held it up to the light and examined it. "It will fetch a good price and repay me for my care of you. Where did you get it?" she asked Sylva.

Sylva tried to tell them of the ribbon and the river, the tall woman and the black crevasse. But they laughed at her and did not believe her. Yet they could not explain away the jewel. So they left her then and went off to the city to sell it. When they returned, it was late. They thrust Sylva outside to sleep and went themselves to their comfortable beds to dream of their new riches.

Sylva sat on the cold ground and thought about what had happened. She reached up and took down the ribbon from her hair. She stroked it, and it felt smooth and soft and yet hard, too. Carefully she placed it on the ground.

In the moonlight, the ribbon glittered and shone. Sylva recalled the song she had heard, so she sang it to herself:

> *Silver ribbon, silver hair,*
> *Carry Sylva with great care,*
> *Bring my daughter home.*

Suddenly the ribbon began to grow and change, and there at her feet was a silver highway that glittered and glistened in the moonlight.

Without a moment's hesitation, Sylva got up and stepped out onto the road and waited for it to bring her to the magical house.

But the road did not move.

"Strange," she said to herself. "Why does it not carry me as the river did?"

Sylva stood on the road and waited a moment more, then tentatively set one foot in front of the other. As soon as she had set off on her own, the road set off, too, and they moved together past fields and forests, faster and faster, till the scenery seemed to fly by and blur into a moon-bleached rainbow of yellows, grays, and black.

The road took a great turning and then quite suddenly stopped, but Sylva did not. She scrambled up the bank where the road ended and found herself again in the meadow. At the far rim of the grass, where the forest began, was the house she had seen before.

Sylva strode purposefully through the grass, and this time the meadow was filled with the song of birds, the meadowlark and the bunting and the sweet jug-jug-jug of the nightingale. She could smell fresh-mown hay and the pungent pine.

The door of the house stood wide open, so Sylva went right in. The long hall was no longer dark but filled with the strange moonglow. And when she reached the crystal door at the end, and gazed at her reflection twelve times in the glass, she saw her own face set with strange gray eyes and long gray hair. She put her hand up to her mouth to stop herself from crying out. But the sound came through, and the door opened of itself.

Inside was the tall woman, all in white, and the globe above her was as bright as a harvest moon.

"Welcome, my sister," the woman said.

"I have no sister," said Sylva, "but the two stepsisters I left at home. And you are none of those."

"I am if you make me so."

"How do I do that?"

"Give me back my heart which you took from me yesterday."

"I did not take your heart. I took nothing but a crystal jewel."

The woman smiled. "It was my heart."

Sylva looked stricken. "But I cannot give it back. My stepmother took it from me."

"No one can take unless you give."

"I had no choice."

"There is always a choice," the woman said.

Sylva would have cried then, but a sudden thought struck her. "Then it must have been your choice to give me your heart."

The woman smiled again, nodded gently, and held out her hand.

Sylva placed her hand in the woman's and there glowed for a moment on the woman's breast a silvery jewel that melted and disappeared.

"Now will you give me your heart?"

"I have done that already," said Sylva, and as she said it, she knew it to be true.

The woman reached over and touched Sylva on her breast and her heart sprang out onto the woman's hand and turned into two fiery red jewels. "Once given, twice gained," said the woman. She handed one of the jewels back to Sylva. "Only take care that you give each jewel with love."

Sylva felt the jewel warm and glowing in her hand and at its touch felt such comfort as she had not in many days. She closed her eyes and a smile came on her face. And when she opened her eyes again, she was standing on the meadow grass not two steps from her own door. It was morning, and by her feet lay the silver ribbon, limp and damp from the frost.

The door to her house stood open.

Sylva drew in her breath, picked up the ribbon, and went in.

"What has happened to your hair?" asked one stepsister.

"What has happened to your eyes?" asked the other.

For indeed Sylva's hair and eyes had turned as silver as the moon.

But the stepmother saw only the fiery red jewel in Sylva's hand. "Give it to me," she said, pointing to the gem.

At first Sylva held out her hand, but then quickly drew it back. "I *can* not," she said.

The stepmother's eyes became hard. "Girl, give it here."

"I *will* not," said Sylva.

The stepmother's eyes narrowed. "Then you shall tell me where you got it."

"That I shall, and gladly," said Sylva. She told them of the silver ribbon and the silver road, of the house with the crystal door. But strange to say, she left out the woman and her words.

The stepmother closed her eyes and thought. At last she said, "Let me see this wondrous silver ribbon, that I may believe what you say."

Sylva handed her the ribbon, but she was not fooled by her stepmother's tone.

The moment the silver ribbon lay prickly and limp in the stepmother's hand, she looked up triumphantly at Sylva. Her face broke into a wolfish grin. "Fool," she said, "the magic is herein. With this ribbon there are jewels for the taking." She marched out of the door and the stepsisters hurried behind her.

Sylvia walked after them, but slowly, stopping in the open door.

The stepmother flung the ribbon down. In the early morning sun it glowed as if with a cold flame.

"Say the words, girl," the stepmother commanded.

From the doorway Sylva whispered:

> *Silver ribbon, silver hair,*
> *Lead the ladies with great care,*
> *Lead them to their home.*

The silver ribbon wriggled and writhed in the sunlight, and as they watched, it turned into a silver-red stair that went down into the ground.

"Wait," called Sylva. "Do not go." But it was too late.

With a great shout, the stepmother gathered up her skirts and ran down the steps, her daughters fast behind her. And before Sylva could move, the ground had closed up after them and the meadow was as before.

On the grass lay the silver ribbon, limp and dull. Sylva went over and picked it up. As she did so, the jewel melted in her hand and she felt a burning in her breast. She put her hand up to it, and she felt her heart beating strongly beneath. Sylva smiled, put the silver ribbon in her pocket, and went back into her house.

After a time, Sylva's hair returned to its own color, except for seven silver strands, but her eyes never changed back. And when she was married and had a child of her own, Sylva plucked the silver strands from her own hair and wove them into the silver ribbon, which she kept in a wooden box. When Sylva's child was old enough to understand, the box with the ribbon was put into her safekeeping, and she has kept them for her own daughter to this very day.

This is all true. I cannot read the letter aloud without tearing up. When I read it at the end of speeches, the entire audience is awash.

The Story Between

When I am in my fiat-issuing mood, I am tempted to announce that there is no one right way to read a story. Only, I add under my breath, plenty of wrong ways to teach it. That is because there is no real story on the page, only that which is created in between the writer and the reader.

Just as the writer brings a lifetime to the creation of the tale, so the reader carries along a different lifetime with which to recreate it. Even the author may reread her own story days, weeks, months later and understand it on another level. I once wrote a poem called "The Storyteller" (proving again that I am always smartest when I am writing and not when I am thinking):

> A story must be worn again
> before the magic garment
> fits the ready heart.

Thus, there is no way an author can write to an audience. Oh, perhaps we may — as they say in faerie — be *guiled* about audience profile for a while. We may be tempted to write for that mythical "5–7 year old" or "8–12 year old," each as wily a shape-shifter as ever roamed the unicorn's garden. But there is only one real audience for the writer of tales, the child within.

How can I be sure that each reader has a hand in the creation of a tale, shaped to his or her own "ready heart"? I can only offer as proof the many letters and confrontations of stories that I have had over a twenty-year span. The storyteller in California who tells me a young couple chose to have my story "Dawn Strider" told at their wedding. "Dawn Strider"? It is a tale about a giant who steals the sun. Or the college student who asked her professor if my story "The Lady and the Merman" was about taking drugs. And this a fairy tale about a unloved young woman who dives after a merman into the sea. Then there was the young woman who, after hearing my story "The Face in the Cloth," was able to say the name of her famous mother out loud and start her own life. And the line in my own story "The Boy Who Sang for Death," written ten years after my own mother died: "Any gift I have I would give to get my mother back." When I reread that line, some months after having penned it, I began to weep, bringing to a close a long-drawn-out formal mourning period.

Therapy? Healing? Self-recognition? The "holistic" powers of stories have long been part of the ritual of tale telling. And today many therapists are using stories with their patients. But I am not talking about that. It is merely that we *bring* to tales that most complex of constructs — ourselves. And we *take* from them what we need. It is as true with the writer as the reader.

When I wrote "The Girl Who Loved the Wind," I wrote it with two emotional agendas, one I recognized at the time, one I understood only long after. That is not an unusual occurrence with my stories. I wrote about a girl who was overprotected, bound in, literally, by the walls of her father's great house and kept a prisoner of his desire to save her from the evils of the world. So it had been, figuratively, with my own father. But the story is also about a wind that blows in over the garden wall and tells the young woman about the ever-changing world. And in the end, she chooses to leave her father's house by spreading her cloak on the ocean, lifting one end, and being blown out into that world by the wind. It took me years to realize, to remember that, when I met my husband, he climbed in the window of the first-floor apartment I shared with two other girls in Greenwich Village. It was during a party where so many of our friends were standing in line at the door, that this enterprising young man took a shortcut. "The Girl Who Loved the Wind" memorializes that meeting in a metaphoric way.

But years later a child came to that tale with another agenda altogether. Her way of hearing that story was as "right," was as valid, as any other. Yet had I tried to write a story *for* her, I would have failed, awash in sentiment and tears. I heard of Ann Marie through a letter from a stranger:

Nov. 7, 1984

Dear Jane:

I was working at a children's hospital as the person coordinating the child activity program. My main work with patients was to be with children who were gravely ill, having chemotherapy, or in some other way needing real support. I often used play therapy techniques or puppets, but if children were too sick I would read to them.

Ann Marie was an eleven-year-old girl who had been admitted by a doctor who didn't usually work with us. She had been sick for quite a while but not diagnosed, so by the time her therapy started, she had many tumors. As the therapy started to kill the tumors, her kidneys and then cardiac system were also affected, so that she had to be transferred to the ICU.

It appeared that she had always been an iso-

lated and protected child and the nurses referred to her as "young for her age."

The day I was to see her I was apprehensive. The times I had been in before she had been so sick and was filled with IVs and tubes and monitors. It was hard to think about the person inside that ailing repository of technology. I picked at random a couple of books from the shelf and went down to ICU.

At first all I could think of was how sick she was. Her eyes were half open and her skin was yellow. She hardly moved except to turn her eyes toward me when I came in. I was in gown and mask, as were all three nurses there. They were just finishing her peritoneal dialysis and preparing to leave.

I asked her what she would like me to read and she didn't answer. "Would you like me to choose?" She nodded.

And then, Jane, when I started reading "The Girl Who Loved the Wind" the whole scene changed. The humming and beeping machines receded; the fear and pain stepped back into the corners of the room; I read this child a story that was all about her life and leaving.

She was a child who had grown up behind protective walls. She too had felt the summons of the wind. "Not always good, not always kind" and was deciding to leave her overly protected life.

When I finished reading the story, we just sat for a while in silence.

Two days later she was dead, her doctor and family shocked because it seemed so sudden, not expected. The date she died was Nov. 5.

I have always since then loved that story. I went to the ICU to search for it, but it was gone. It wasn't until two years later, to the day, that I found it again.

I know it truly served to comfort the departure of that child.

The morning after her death, after we had cried and talked and wept about it, a beautiful stellar jay flew into our patio, came and sat on the arm of a chair and looked into the bedroom at me, still in bed. He sat there almost a minute and I was filled then with a sense of peace. He seemed to say, "I come from Ann Marie and she's alright now."

These are things that you should know.

So two people met, with a story between them. The story I wrote was not exactly the story that Ann Marie took with her. But she took it with her because she needed it and I am not so selfish about the meaning of my tales to deny all the Ann Maries in the world that garment for the trip.

Editor's Acknowledgments

The text for virtually all of the stories and essays in this book was scanned by Frank & Lisa Richards of Quick Scan, Inc. (PO Box 71, Marlow, NH 03456; 603-446-7307), for which we are immensely grateful. Our first-round proofreaders were Claire Anderson, Ann Broomhead, Gay Ellen Dennett, George Flynn, Pam Fremon, Deb Geisler, Merle Insinga, Sue Kahn, 'Zanne Labonville, Paula Lieberman, Rich Maynard, Mark Olson, Kelly Persons, Sharon Sbarsky, Charlie Seelig, Tim Szczesuil, and Pat Vandenberg. Our second-round proofreaders were Pam Fremon and Priscilla Olson. As usual, our final proofreader was the irreplaceable George Flynn. Our contract negotiator and speaker-to-printers was Mark Olson. Our author liaison was Priscilla Olson, aided by GEnie. Research was provided by Claire Anderson, George Flynn, and Pam Fremon. Editorial assistance was provided by Pam Fremon. Critical technical assistance was provided by Jim Mann, Mark Olson, and Greg Thokar.

Special thanks go to Gay Ellen Dennett and Priscilla Olson for their support, and to Merle Insinga for reasons too numerous to mention.

Aron Insinga, Editor
Nashua, NH
7 December 1991

This book was set by Aron Insinga in Adobe's rendition of Goudy Old Style using Microsoft Word 4.0 and Aldus PageMaker 4.01 on a Macintosh SE/30, and printed on Neutral pH 60# Natural Smooth paper and bound by Braun-Brumfield, Inc., of Ann Arbor, Michigan from camera-ready copy generated at 130% on a Tegra 1000dpi printer.